G000131271

Murdoch

Also by CJ Matthew

The Colonel's Daughters, A Quintet

A Major Seduction
Compromising the Captain

The Paladin Group

Deadly Reboot
Survival Reboot
Maximum Reboot

Dolphin Shore Shifters Series

Blood Tide
Risky Tide
Dangerous Tide
Lethal Tide
Toxic Tide

CJ Matthew

Murdoch

Book One in the Sea Dragon Shifters series

Murdoch
Published by All Huston Group, Inc.
Copyright 2018 by All Huston Group, Inc.
Cover copyright 2018 by Sharon Lipman at Fantasia Covers
ISBN paperback: 978-0-9994640-1-4

All rights reserved. Without limiting the rights under copyright reserved above, no part of this publication may be reproduced, stored in or introduced into a retrieval system, or transmitted, in any form, or by any means (electronic, mechanical, photocopying, recording, or otherwise) without the prior written permission of both the copyright owner and the above publisher of this book.

This is a work of fiction. Names, characters, places, brands, media, and incidents are either the product of the author's imagination or are used fictitiously. The author acknowledges the trademarked status and trademark owners of various products referenced in this work of fiction, which have been used without permission. The publication/use of these trademarks is not authorized, associated with, or sponsored by the trademark owners.

This book is licensed for your personal enjoyment only and **may not be re-sold**. Thank you for respecting the author's time and work.

www.cjmatthew.com

Chapter One

Murdoch raced along the upstairs hallway, rounding the corner at almost his full human speed, and nearly collided with his twin brother striding quickly toward him from the opposite direction.

"Where've you been?" Murdoch demanded as Murphy reached his side and stopped. "We're going to be late."

"Long distance call," Murphy said cryptically, and pocketed the satellite phone he'd been holding.

After a quick peek at his watch, Murdoch studied his brother. He'd recognize that stressed expression anywhere. Evidence of worry was all too common on his twin's face. *Damn it.* The last thing he needed was to get stuck running the quarterly meeting all by himself. Better hustle big brother downstairs. *Now.*

Halfway down the main staircase, he surrendered to his pang of guilt and asked, "What's wrong?"

"I have to leave, right now," Murphy announced with a deeper frown. "Emergency summons to…um,

Ireland."

Oh, Hell no. Murdoch stopped on the bottom stair and scowled. His brother's actual destination *could be* Ireland since the family corporation had been founded there centuries ago. However, all their port facilities in Ireland were thriving. What secret *emergency* could they be having that required the company president to drop everything and go today?

Murdoch stepped down, moved closer to his brother, and lowered his voice to a whisper. "The druids?"

"That's right," Murphy whispered back. "For the time I'm on their island, I'll be totally unreachable." As they started across the foyer together, he shot Murphy a sidelong glance. As usual, his brother's brow was creased, his lips compressed into a thin line. The man's default expression these days was strained, harried. *There but for a twist of fate, go I.*

Just over a century ago, his twin had emerged from their shared egg several minutes ahead of Murdoch, which meant that decades later, when their parents had been killed, his brother had become the chieftain of the clan, president of Muirdris Shipping, and one of the shifter guardians of a secret island north of Ireland where the ancient druids were hidden and protected from hunters.

Murphy pulled out his iPhone and checked it as they drew closer to the front door. "My housekeeper is taking care of my place, I've alerted the staff at headquarters in Boston. The helicopter is airborne, en route here. It'll drop me off at Logan and I'll be taking the corporate jet."

Halfway across his marble floored entry area, Murdoch extended his arm to stop his brother. "Thanks for smoothing the way for me to enjoy an uneventful week in your absence, but what about the quarterly directors meeting?" He dropped his gaze to the floor. "The one starting in eleven minutes."

"You'll have to handle it alone."

Oh no. *Damn it.* The pit of Murdoch's stomach clenched like an electric eel was fighting its way out. "Wait. You staying here a few more minutes won't make any difference. Together we can knock out this meeting in, say, half an hour, and then—"

"You'll have to do this one, little brother, without me." Murphy detoured around him and reached for the front door handle. "Considering today's agenda, you'd better plan on the whole deal running closer to three hours."

"*What?* No, listen..." Murdoch pleaded, "We'll flip for it. If I win, you stay just long enough to get through the old business." Which should mean Murphy would deal with the worst of the contentious dragon-eat-dragon debates and the most difficult decisions.

When his brother didn't respond, Murdoch wedged himself between his twin's powerful body and the door and he drew an old coin from his pocket. Flicking the Celtic piece with his thumb, Murdoch sent the artifact arching into the air. "Call it," he urged Murphy as the ancient money flipped end over end.

"Heads," Murphy said without looking up from his phone.

The coin landed back in Murdoch's waiting hand. "Heads," he groaned. "Shit." He glared at the coin, then at his brother. "Best two out of three?"

"No chance." Murphy reached around him to open the door. "I've got a flight to catch. You've got a teleconference to run. Even I can't be in two places at the same time."

Murdoch followed his twin outside into the early afternoon chill and across the gravel driveway, carefully pocketing the coin until he could restore it to his hoard. Wearing or carrying small but significant pieces from his treasure usually brought him good luck. *Not today.* Bringing this particular item out of the secret cave beneath his house had been a spur-of-the-moment decision. Taking into account the added expense he'd incurred by legally buying the coin, it was almost too valuable to risk.

As grey storm clouds rolled across the sky above the lawn, the Muirdris helicopter lowered onto the landing pad.

"Quit pouting, brother, I won fair and square," Murphy reminded him. "However, I'm not the least concerned. I believe you can handle the quarterly conference and whatever else comes up while I'm gone. I trust you'll keep the company prospering. Oh, don't forget to show up for the christening ceremony of our newest container vessel."

All through the routine meaningless reassurances, Murphy's gaze kept wandering to Murdoch's hand buried in his pants pocket. Finally, his older brother looked him in the eye and asked, "Where'd you get the coin?"

Murdoch's mood brightened, and he bit back a smile. This was why he'd taken a risk, brought the precious coin out of his hoard for the day. Hell, this was why he'd bought the coin in the first place. He'd never felt equal to his brother when it came to the business or his handling of the cousins, but Murdoch knew his history and he was able to find amazing and unique additions to his already impressive personal hoard. It was the one—possibly the *only*—talent of his that his twin envied. Murphy's question about the origin of the piece might sound nonchalant, but Murdoch wasn't fooled. Tightening his grip on the treasure, he remained silent as the ancient metal warmed his hand.

"It's from the Isle of Jersey archeological find, isn't it?" Murphy pressed for an answer.

Murdoch shrugged. "It belongs to my hoard now," he retorted and bit back a laugh. When digging for information, his brother was like a Terrier going after a rat, but Murdoch wasn't about to share how he'd acquired the coin. *Time to change the subject.*

"Tell the truth," he demanded. "How many nasty surprises should I expect during this teleconference?"

"You mean," Murphy said, "besides the constant in-fighting between the cousins? As far as I know, none. There shouldn't be any bombshells."

They exchanged a back-slapping hug, and when he drew back, Murphy's elusive smile appeared. "Not to worry, baby twin."

"Don't call me that." Murdoch winced. He hated the childhood nickname.

Murphy's gaze hardened again as he assumed his business face. Then he turned and strolled toward the concrete square set in the side lawn. Despite the rotor noise, Murdoch heard his twin mutter under his breath, "If you're serious about proving yourself, little brother, there's no time like the present."

He drew in a sharp breath, but before he could respond, Murphy had moved out of earshot, and Murdoch's watch beeped. *Seven minutes.* Shrugging off the remark, he waved to the pilot and shouted at his brother's back, "Have a safe journey." Then he reentered his house to face the corporate directors alone.

He and Murphy took turns electronically hosting Muirdris Shipping's monthly meetings and the quarterly teleconferences from their nearby clifftop estates north of Boston. The two properties were located far enough apart to satisfy their dragons territorial demands, similar enough to make their twin natures happy yet not identical like their human forms.

As befitted the clan chief, Murphy's domain boasted more acreage, higher cliffs, the spacious mansion had more square footage and was located several miles closer to Boston. Only the secure communication facilities secreted in each basement, chock full of the latest electronics, and protected by the newest security devises, were identical.

Murdoch hurried down the circular stone staircase, an exact replica of the medieval stairs built to access the defensive towers of their clan castle in Ireland. Exiting on the first landing, he used the palm ID and retinal scanner to gain entry to his conference room. Once inside, he carefully locked the reinforced door behind him.

Especially for these quarterly conferences, absolute security was a must. Muirdris Shipping's fourth quarter global teleconference would include discussions of ongoing as well as new security threats, followed by in-depth analyses of how Muirdris would respond. Finally, the worldwide directors, his cousins, would vote on year-end acquisitions and final annual budget issues.

During the debate on acquisitions, the directors were expecting a positive progress report from him. Last quarter, he'd been 'offered' the chance to broker a deal with a financially troubled Greek shipping line, Mykos. A buy-out sounded great, until his careful research revealed that Mykos wasn't just broke, their debt ratio was fatal. To make the transaction profitable, he'd have to convince the owners of Mykos Lines to carve out one division and sell it. Hampered by the need for secrecy, so far he hadn't made much progress.

Inside the secure room, the decor abruptly switched from medieval Celtic to ultra-futuristic. From this sleekly efficient space, he could contact each of Muirdris' vessels, every port and corporate office and all the sea dragon shifter cousins who managed the worldwide operations.

On the far wall, a huge computer screen would project live feed of each participant, while the center portion handled PowerPoint presentations, or maps, outlines, or photos relevant to the current topic.

As he watched, their two most trusted non-dragon employees from Muirdris Shipping's corporate Boston headquarters appeared on the screen. Victoria, a brilliant and stunningly beautiful blue-eyed blonde, the vice president of global electronic communications and an arctic fox shifter sat at her command console. Seated at his own sleek curved desk in a different secure room in Boston, Gahaji a tall, muscular, ebony skinned jaguar shifter, and vice president of Muirdris' worldwide security, glanced up and smiled a greeting.

"Good afternoon," Victoria and Gahaji said in unison.

"Hey Vic, Ji," Murdoch called over his shoulder as he filled a glass with iced water while his mug of coffee brewed. Turning to face the screen, Murdoch hesitated a split second before he placed the water on a coaster and set his mug beside it. Then he pulled out Murphy's chair front and center at the expansive glass and chrome table. Once he was settled, he took a swallow of coffee, and looked at the two shifters on the screen.

"Murphy?" Vic asked hesitantly.

Murdoch frowned. He couldn't fool the corporate staff—not for long, anyway. "No," he said, "Murphy's been called away." He took another sip of coffee. "Just me today...and for at least the next week," he muttered the last part under his breath.

Familiar faces began to pop up along the edges of the wall screen as far-flung directors joined the conference.

"Hey," Devlin in Japan called out, waving frantically for attention. "Hello, Murph? Sorry to disrupt the agenda. Where's Murdoch? I need to share a serious security breach. I had—"

"Murphy isn't here," Vic announced. "You're talking to Murdoch."

He sipped coffee and listened to the surprised silence all around. Finally, Devlin gave an exaggerated shrug, and said, "Okay, no sweat. This concerns you the most. Just before this meeting, I had an unexpected visitor. The man said he was a representative from Mykos, that Greek shipping line you're negotiating with? You know, the one we've *secretly* discussed buying? When I asked him what he wanted, he claimed to know we're interested in acquiring them."

What the fuck? Murdoch sat bolt upright in his chair. How could that happen? The news was met by several colorful profanities and lots of grumbling from the other directors.

"Did it ever occur to you, Devlin, that he might've been bluffing?" Finnian, the sea dragon in charge of the US west coast ports asked from the secure room in the Seattle offices. His mouth was set in a sneer. "I'll bet the Greek guy was simply fishing for information and you, dumbass, gave it to him."

"Like hell I did," Devlin's voice rose. "Before I had a chance to give anything away, Mr. Zor informed me he'd learned about our interest directly from a Muirdris source."

The reactions grew so loud, Murdoch raised one hand for silence. As usual, everybody ignored him. So much for no bombshells. *Damn it.* He sucked in a deep breath and released a painfully shrill whistle. That got their attention.

Wordlessly, he motioned for Devlin to continue.

"The Greek man, Mr. Zor," Devin said, "refused to name his source, but he was insistent it was a current Muirdris employee. Based on news of our interest, the asking price for Mykos has sky-rocketed. Guys, we've got a dangerous and expensive leak in our company."

As all hell broke loose, Murdoch gritted his teeth.

Chapter Two

With thirty seconds to spare, Annalisa Bartello slid into her office chair at Muirdris Shipping's Port of Long Beach facility. Firing up her desk computer, she clocked-in while she added one more packet of sugar to her 30oz. tumbler of strong coffee. Stirring with one hand, she opened her work email with the other. After a long swallow of sugary caffeine, Annalisa blinked at the inbox list, her eyes gritty from lack of sleep.

One email immediately caught her attention. It was addressed to ABartellino and came from an unfamiliar sender. Hesitant to open it, she ran a search through the corporate employee alphabetical listings and confirmed that Muirdris, including their port facilities in Italy, did not employ a person named Bartellino. The closest name listed was hers.

The sender had used the company server. And netiquette urged her to notify whoever was at the sending address that his or her email had been misdirected. The subject line simply read *Our Deal.* She opened the body of the message, searching for a name. Her cursor hovered over the reply button while she read a terse offer to sell confidential docking protocols from three of Muirdris Shipping's most active ports.

Annalisa gasped, horrified at the implied security breach. She reread the final paragraph.

"This offer has a strict time limit. Reply with confirmation of payment by 23:55 Pacific Standard today or this offer will go to another."

Annalisa's stomach churned. She bent forward, her head between her knees until the dizziness subsided. Damn the nightmares. She needed a clear head to deal with this.

Six weeks ago, her boss, Finnian had offered her a terrific promotion. Because the new job description placed her on two of Muirdris' top secret port expansion projects, she'd been required to pass a deep background check to qualify. No problem. She didn't have any skeletons in her closets.

A few weeks later, her higher security clearance had come through. She'd been awarded the promotion, had begun attending secret project meetings, and she'd celebrated the nice pay increase by taking the non-work friends, her beach volleyball team, out for drinks.

Oddly, when the background check concluded,

she'd started to experience vague, unnerving dreams. She tossed and turned, feeling an urgent need to locate someone, without knowing who, exactly, or why. In her dream sequence last night, she'd searched a deserted stretch of beach and when her dream-self dove into the surf, swimming in the general direction of Catalina, she'd started awake and fought her way out of the tangled sheets.

How did her unconscious come up with this shit?

Usually her dreams offered up tidbits from her day or week which she could easily identify. Were these uncomfortable imaginings about work? No way. She loved the excitement of her job, working for family-owned, employee friendly Muirdris.

At least she had, until today. Now she was confronted with a genuine security breach. A conspirator at Muirdris was going to sell corporate protocols. *Tonight.*

It was her duty to tell someone. *Now.*

The obvious choice was Finnian, her immediate supervisor. The drawback? As the West Coast Director, the man travelled—a lot. Yesterday afternoon, for example, he'd left the office early, headed to the Seattle facilities for several days of meetings.

She had to call him.

Her computer signaled the arrival of a new email.

On her screen was a second misdirected message. From the same mysterious sender. *Holy hell.*

This subject line read: *Sample.* And the email had an attachment.

She rubbed the crop of goosebumps spreading up her arms, took a deep breath, and opened the accompanying document.

It appeared to be a scanned copy of a paper original. She shivered. Originally printed on a Muirdris interoffice memo, the document was clearly stamped TOP SECRET. Several crucial columns were blacked out, but this *sample* was solid proof that someone at Muirdris had access to confidential data and that someone was willing to sell out the company.

Grabbing the handset for the landline, she paused. If she could get through to Finnian, would he and Muirdris want her repeating this kind of sensitive news over the phone? The damn email system had already proven fallible.

Annalisa scraped her front teeth across her lower lip. What choice did she have? Maybe if she hinted at the problem, Finnian would arrange a more secure way for her to inform him.

She didn't make it past Finnian's personal assistant in Seattle.

"I'm sorry, Annalisa," the older woman said,

"Finnian has been in meetings since dawn. One more and then we're setting up for the big worldwide tele-conference. I can give the boss your message when that's concluded."

"This is extremely urgent." She racked her brain for ideas, while she tried to slow her breathing. "He needs to get my message soon. Definitely before he goes into that big teleconference. Meanwhile, I'll leave an urgent call-back request on his cell phone voice mail."

Calling his iPhone, she was sent directly to voice mail. "Finnian, this is Annalisa. I need to speak to you about a critical, time sensitive matter. Please call me here in Long Beach or on my cell as soon as you get this."

She tagged the message *Urgent*.

Now, two problems remained. Since the system wouldn't allow her to forward or copy the incriminat-ing emails, how could she preserve the evidence? And how could she get said evidence to Finnian in Seattle?

Still gripping her iPhone, she had a brainstorm. Take pictures of the emails and the attachment. Then Finnian could figure out how to access the originals and backtrack to uncover the real name and location of the sender.

After saving the photographs in her phone, she

closed the connection to the Muirdris server. And glanced at her Felix the Cat wall clock. 9:25 a.m. Time to try Finnian again.

What if she still couldn't get through to him? She needed a backup plan. Who else could she call? At least one person at Muirdris was a traitor. Maybe more than one. Hell, she was scared enough, tired enough, and paranoid enough to suspect damn near everyone.

Maybe she needed to aim higher? Figure out which Muirdris *executive* she could bring herself to trust. She'd always considered herself a good judge of people, especially when she could look a person in the eye. Not happening. The only Muirdris big shot on this side of the U.S. was Finnian. The only east coast employee she knew, via phone, was Victoria in tech support. Not exactly executive level.

She experienced a replay of the heart pounding fear and dread from last night. Damn, there was a hell of a lot at stake here. If she contacted the wrong person, was it possible both she and the emails would simply disappear?

Cut the drama and concentrate. The longer it took Finnian to return her call, the more she needed an alternate plan. Shaking the tension out of her hands, Annalisa accessed the corporate listings in search of Victoria. No one with that name in Support.

Wait, there was a Victoria in the Communications department...*Oh my god.* A vice president based in Boston. No, there had to be another one.

There wasn't. The chatty tech support woman Annalisa had reached on the help line that Saturday after the office phone line went dead? The woman was a VP.

Annalisa cross-checked again, just to be sure.

Since she couldn't look into Victoria's eyes, maybe a photo would help decide?

Re-opening her browser, she skimmed for pictures of Victoria. *Nada.* Searching through Muirdris annual reports, and worldwide newsletters, she ran across *The Muirdris Story.* And chuckled. The first time she'd heard it, in orientation, she remembered thinking it sounded like a Celtic fable.

Muirdris Shipping had been founded in Ireland ages ago by the Rudraige Family. Soon after the Pilgrims landed on Plymouth Rock, it expanded to establish headquarters in Boston. *Jeez.* Why not claim the Ark was a Muirdris ship?

Still no images of Victoria.

She plowed through internet gossip about the owner of Muirdris, Murphy Rudraige. Most of the stories used the same stilted photograph. The man was movie-star handsome, yet seriously allergic to cameras?

Finally, she uncovered a photo spread on Muirdris published a decade ago in a glossy Japanese magazine. She'd couldn't read the captions. Instead, she scrolled through pictures of Muirdris container ships, the offices in Japan, and found a different pose of Murphy Rudraige standing with several other hunks in suits. Below a brief article in Japanese, was one picture, taken with a telephoto lens, of a stone mansion perched on a cliff overlooking the ocean. The Rudraige Estate in Massachusetts.

Her head buzzed with caffeine overload. She checked for a call back from Finnian. Nothing. It was decision time. What would her late mother advise?

"Darling, you're letting that vivid imagination of yours run away with your common sense. Go ahead and forward the emails to someone in security. Get back to work on your job."

Screw that. A potential disaster for her employer had landed in her inbox. She wasn't about to forward the responsibility and hope for the best.

Annalisa pulled up a budget airline website to price tickets. *Holy shit*. A seat on the midday flight from Long Beach, California to Boston's Logan International would literally empty her savings account.

She stared at the screen, chewing on her bottom lip. Sure, the person sending the email had set a deadline to respond. Was that enough to trigger the acute sense of urgency she felt? Damn, she was one click away from totally emptying her hard-won savings account.

Holding her breath, she pressed *Purchase*. And immediately, a wave of giddy relief swept over her. Relief that was way out of proportion. What was drawing her to the east coast? She admired Murphy Rudraige in the photo she'd seen, still, she wasn't attracted to him.

She pre-checked-in online and printed her ticket. Gripping the boarding pass, she vowed, after she rescued Muirdris, she'd file for reimbursement on the ticket. She sent an online request for personal leave, starting immediately, to Finnian and HR. Then she raced home to pack and catch a ride to the airport.

In the departure terminal, her phone rang.

"Hey Liz."

"What's the fuck is going on?" Her best friend could be short on tact.

"I won't be at volleyball practice tomorrow. Business trip to Boston. Boarding in a few minutes."

"I call bullshit. Your job doesn't have business trips. What are you up to now?"

"Can't give you details over the phone, but my trip *is* for Muirdris. Meeting with the VP of Communications in the Boston corporate office."

"I knew it. Delusions of grandeur."

"I may end up seeing the company president."

"My ass. Be careful, Annalisa, and I beg you, for once in your life, try looking before you leap."

Annalisa disconnected and smiled. *Too late.* Besides, at this point, she pictured herself in the role of heroine, a woman on a mission. She might single-handedly save Muirdris.

Since it was her first trip to Massachusetts, to compliment the cheapest car she could rent at Boston airport, she forked over extra for a portable GPS unit. That baby paid for itself leading her from Logan to the Muirdris corporate offices overlooking Boston Harbor.

Unfortunately, the computerized voice didn't offer bargain parking advice and she drove around an extra thirty minutes looking for a place to park that didn't charge big bucks for fractions of minutes.

She hiked the long blocks to Muirdris and managed to sneak past the lobby security guard to the elevator banks. On the floor designated Communications, she was greeted by a slender, dark-haired receptionist.

"How may I help you?"

"Hello. I'd like to speak with Victoria. I don't have an appointment but I 'm sure she'll want to see me."

"Your name?" the young woman smiled.

Crap. She really didn't want to tell these people she was an employee. With a sinking stomach, she told the receptionist her name.

After a moment the woman was back, "Victoria is still in the teleconference but her personal assistant, Darren will see you."

And again, decision time. She didn't want to talk to the assistant of a person she didn't really know. "Okay." She'd have to ditch this woman before they got to Darren.

"I'll escort you to his office."

Annalisa followed the woman deeper into the labyrinth of office space until she spotted a rest room. "Excuse me. I need to use the ladies. I'll be right out, or you could just point me from here."

"It's right around the corner." Her smile faltered. "However, I'd better wait for you."

More trust issues. Annalisa took her time. When she slowly cracked open the door to the hall, her escort was angled away, leaning against the far wall, and engrossed in her iPhone. Slipping out, she hurriedly tiptoed around the corner. Down the hall, she spotted an shiny plaque with Victoria's name and Vice President of Communications.

The door wasn't completely closed, and creeping closer, she overheard a man on the phone. The hair on the back of her neck stood up. He was sharing details of a top-secret port security project she was familiar with. He called the person he was speaking to Ji. Who was Ji?

Hurrying past the doorway, she turned the corner at the far end of the hall and circled back to the elevators. She rode up as many floors as she could without an executive keycard.

The elevator doors slid open to a noticeably fancier floor. She swept past the empty reception counter then only made it a few steps into a plush common area when she was stopped dead by another assistant.

She tried to charm him, but when he assured her that Murphy wasn't in the building, she believed him and left promptly.

Back in the car, she muttered, "What the hell." Jokingly she typed *Rudraige Estate* into the GPS. The machine not only recognized the name, it also supplied the estate's exact address. The computerized voice confidently led her north of Boston, up along the coast and then miles down a remote, windy road before it announced, *Recalculating, recalculating…* No matter what buttons she pressed, the GPA insisted it was *Recalculating.* Finally, she'd turned it off in disgust.

Slowing the vehicle to a crawl, she scowled up at the dark clouds. Flicking the headlights from high beam to low and back again, she couldn't discern any difference in visibility. *Crap. This was her last option.* She had to find the mansion. Had to locate Murphy and warn him.

Still peering through the windshield, she searched the deserted two-lane highway for a road sign. Any sign, really, that would offer a clue as to where, exactly, she was.

"Damn." Disgusted with the GPS and frustrated by her lack of progress, Annalisa pulled over to the side of the road. Leaning back against the headrest, she closed her eyes and wished for an oversized mug of sweet, hot coffee.

Her eyes flew open. No wonder she was drooping. Low blood sugar. She hadn't eaten. She rummaged through her over-sized purse and wolfed down a bag of peanuts. Then she lingered over a candy bar and polished off the water she'd replenished in the Communications floor rest room.

The chocolate kicked in. She apologized to the

GPS for her stupidity, erased *Rudraige Estate* and instead, typed in the full address the machine had supplied earlier. She watched the map materialize and grinned when the voice said, *continue to highlighted route.* She let out a whoop when the GPS said, *arrive at destination in nine minutes.*

Right on time, she turned into a spacious driveway and stopped at an ornate wrought iron gate, still debating the best way to get past security. She hadn't had much success with Muirdris assistants today, maybe she'd have better luck charming a rent-a-cop in uniform?

Annalisa eyed the spikes atop the gate. If she was turned away here, did she have the guts to climb Murphy's fence?

She jumped when a deep male voice said, "Can I help you?"

"Yes, please." She lowered the window and searched for a camera, a speaker. Where was he? She'd much rather do this face to face. "Where are you?"

"Nearby. This is a private residence. If you tell me your name, I'll see if you're on the list."

"I'm not a guest. I work for Finnian at Muirdris' Long Beach, California facility." She held up her ID badge but wasn't sure where to point it. "This is really urgent. I flew here today hand-carrying extremely confidential information." She held up her airline boarding pass. "I need to deliver it to Murphy Rudraige in person."

"Please wait. I'll need to get authorization for…"

An engine roared behind her, accelerating into the short driveway.

"Brace," the deep voice yelled.

She gripped the wheel and held her breath. A huge vehicle filled the rearview mirror. Smashed into the rear of the rental car. She pitched forward and was flung back as the steering wheel airbag deployed.

Everything went black.

Chapter Three

Murdoch eased back in a padded deck chair, sipping Jamison as he enjoyed the rhythmic crash of the surf onto the rocks below. The living room terrace was one of his favorite spots, perched out over the cliffs and his secret cave. Sitting here, he was as close to the strengthening power of his hoard as he could get in human form. When he felt the urge to exchange an item or occasionally, to sleep on his treasure, he'd shift, and his sea dragon would swim into the tidal cave.

He took a drink and the whiskey left a warm trail down his throat and into his stomach. The sky was dark with clouds and he knew the sun was setting on the other side of the house. Day or night, stormy or clear, the view of the ocean from this terrace was stunning.

As his muscles began to relax, his mind flashed back to the quarterly meeting. He gritted his teeth and his jaw tensed again.

The teleconference had been a never-ending nightmare. The cousins had been on edge, even more so after Devlin's outburst, ready to fight over every damn detail, each fucking expenditure. After three hours listening to them yell, he'd called a halt. Acting like he had the authority to do so, he'd declared the meeting officially closed right in the middle of a spectacular shouting match between Brogan in Germany and Torin in Singapore.

He'd skipped over his report and moved on to today's final agenda item: distribution of the company's third quarter profits. He rolled his eyes. Never again would that be last on the docket. They all knew it was a hot topic. No amount of logic or business wisdom could convince the Rudraige dragons to voluntarily reinvest a penny of Muirdris profit back into Muirdris Shipping. It was a miracle they were still in business.

And the same damn thing happened—with differing levels of animosity—every time profits were discussed. All his cousins wanted to do was divide the money, convert their shares into gold or jewels, and add it to their personal hoards.

He could empathize. He experienced the same urge, but Muirdris belonged to all of them. It represented a major part of the clan's hoard. Investing in new ships, buying out competitors—or parts of competitors—financing port infrastructure and employee retention, and staying current with new technology would gradually pay even bigger profits. Benefiting all of them.

Damn it. He slammed the whiskey glass down on the side table. Next year the First Quarter agenda would *lead off* with profit distributions. And the percentage reinvested back into Muirdris Shipping absolutely would increase. He formed a mental picture of that discussion and chuckled. Good thing he and his dragon cousins were oceans apart. And as hybrid sea serpent dragons, none of them had fire.

Best news of the evening, Fate had granted him an extension on the Mykos deal. Sure, the fact that there might've been a Muirdris leak was bad. Or maybe Mr. Zor had been telling the truth. Simple logic would lead most savvy investors to assume there'd be lots of interest in a failing international business. Sharks circling a wounded competitor.

He'd scheduled a private phone call with Devlin for later tonight—early morning in Japan. He had several follow-up questions about Mr. Zor's unscheduled visit to Devlin. As far as rumors driving the price up—

The sound of a distant crash brought him to his

feet. He pressed the intercom to security. "What happened?"

"Deliberate collision at the front gate, sir. I think the lady will be okay, but the truck that hit her car is driving away."

"Signal for back up. And the doctor. If it's safe to leave her, go after the truck. I'm on my way."

"Yes, sir. Line two."

In the hall Murdoch grabbed one of the Bluetooth earbud/mic sets he'd had Ji customize for internal use on the property, set it on channel two, and ran for the front door.

He met one security guard, armed and alert, stationed just outside the front door.

Murdoch gave him a nod. "Quick update on the crash victim and the truck." He started jogging backwards to hear the reports.

"It's a young woman," the guard talked fast, "26 to 30. Some bruises and cuts. She's conscious and complaining."

"Sounds like a good sign."

"Her rental car is totaled. Unknown truck accelerated, hit it from the rear, and slammed it into the gate."

Ouch. He stopped, looked up at his house. "Anyone try to breach the fence?"

"No sir. The truck reversed, sped away. Without

more data, the woman would appear to be the target."

"Thanks." Murdoch turned and ran toward the crash. "Keep a sharp eye out for intruders," he called over his shoulder.

"Yes, sir."

The front gate had been opened just wide enough for a man to squeeze through. The local retired doctor he kept on retainer for human staff and visitors, pulled his van into the driveway and slid out. "I was on my way home," he explained, and tossed his keys to an approaching watchman. "Medical stuff's inside. Don't move my vehicle until I see what I need."

"Right, Doc." The watchman jiggled the keys and stood by the van's sliding middle door.

Murdoch waved to the white-haired doctor and arrived at the driver's side of the crumpled car just ahead of him. He tapped the arm of the sentry leaning in the car window, "Medic is here."

The guard stood straight and stepped away as the doctor moved forward. Whispering to Murdoch, the sentry said, "Ms. Bartello looks to be banged up a bit otherwise she's in surprisingly good shape. Nothing broken that I can find. She's adamant about no ambulance and insisting she needs to deliver an urgent message to *Murphy* Rudraige."

Well, hell. Wonder what brought her to *my*

house? "All right. Let's see if the Doc is okay with moving her inside."

"Wait sir, the car door is jammed. It'll take a couple of us to pull it open."

He gave the guard's expressionless face a hard look. No one, especially no employees or house staff, knew he and his brother were sea dragon shifters. But over the years, several of his security staff witnessed his better-than-human physical strength. He could help with the door, careful not to appear stronger than a human.

When the doctor smiled and started flirting with the patient, Murdoch knew she wasn't in danger. He pulled out his phone and called Murphy's housekeeper.

"I have an accident victim at my door," he explained. "Could you call the lady who helped out when you had your surgery? See if she can come here right away. Spend a night or two? However long the doctor recommends for a recovery period."

"Certainly, Murdoch, I'll call her now. Alert your team at the gate to expect her and I can have Bridget with you in under an hour. Do you have any food in the house?"

"If Bridget or my guest need anything I don't have, we'll get the grocery and pharmacy to deliver."

"Thank you, sir."

The doctor approached him. "I recommend we transport Ms. Bartello to the hospital but—"

"What's wrong?" He stiffened and took a step toward the woman in the wrecked car.

The doctor tugged his arm. "Slow down, son. She'll be fine. I mentioned the hospital as an alternative to her staying here, since you have an all-male household. The poor woman. How can she be comfortable?"

"Is that your only concern?" His shoulders sagged with relief.

"Well, yes."

"Doctor, I respect your traditional attitude. I've retained a housekeeper, Ms. Bridget. She's on her way here right now to look after our patient and stay as long as you say we need her."

The doctor's light blue eyes widened with surprise, then his creased face beamed with approval. "Good man. Let's get Ms. Bartello out of that wreck. I want two of your strongest men ready to carry her, chair style."

"Or I could carry her myself," Murdoch offered.

"We'll let the lady decide. Best to transfer her to a couch. In a warm room with a fireplace maybe? And a TV? Until Ms. Bridget can get her guest room ready.

Any bedrooms on the main floor?"

"Several." He eyed the fanciful physician. And almost offered to fill Ms. Bartello's room with roses and chocolates. Instead, he bit his tongue. "Let's get the vehicle door open."

He signaled to Ryan, the security supervisor. "We'll need two men familiar with a chair carry. After we get her car door open, they'll carry the patient to the sofa in the library"

"Right, sir." Ryan signaled to another uniformed guard and they stepped forward.

Murdoch ducked his head to peer inside the crumpled car. In profile, the curvy brunette appeared to be biting her bottom lip. Was she blinking back tears? A wave of warmth surged over him. Poor thing. What business did she have with Murphy?

He gently cleared his throat. "Um, Ms. Bartello, I'm Mr. Rudraige. As an employee you're used to first names. Here we're more formal. Please call me Mr. Rudraige, and let me tell you how sorry—"

Her head turned slowly until she faced him. The deep brown eyes *were* moist, but he was no longer certain it was caused by tears. Her eyes widened, and he experienced a wave of dizziness. This close, he could see tiny golden flecks in her irises. Framed by unbelievably long eyelashes. She was the most gorgeous creature he'd ever seen.

"Murphy?" she whispered. "Really? It's been a hell of a day, but I did it. I actually made it."

His dragon raised its head.

Then Ms. Bartello smiled. A radiant smile that curved her luscious lips up and open. Exposing straight white teeth. "I'm Annalisa," she whispered, and her plump cheeks bloomed in a soft shade of pink.

His dragon swirled his long, barbed tail, demanding to get out.

"Murphy," she sighed.

The dragon snorted and rumbled his protest. *We are Murdoch. She is ours. Not Murphy's. Tell her.*

Oh no, *Hell no.* Murdoch lurched straight up and smacked his head on the top of the door frame. "Son of a—"

"You all right, son?" The doctor scooted forward.

What the hell was going on with his crazy dragon? This was no time for dumb Irish fairytales or some cock and bull Celtic tradition about recognizing random women. He rubbed his head. "I'm fine."

Murdoch turned to the grinning guards. "A little help here, with the door." After checking that the door was unlocked, he warned Ms. Bartello, er…Annalisa, to turn her face away. Pointing one guard to each side of the frame, he took the center and gently pulled.

Nothing.

"Let's increase our effort gradually. I don't want strips of metal cutting anyone. Especially not me." The dragon gave him a mental kick in the butt.

"Okay," he muttered. *Got it.* No self-deprecating remarks in front of the lady. But no matter how crazy this beast gets, the woman means nothing to me.

"On three," he said. "One two, pull." The door creaked, and a metal part screeched.

"It's moving," Ryan said. "A little more brute force."

"One, two, pull," Murdoch said. The tearing and screeching made his ears ring, but the door and the top of the frame came off in their hands. Ryan had braced himself and stood his ground. Murdoch and the man on his left staggered back when the door gave way.

He bent forward to make eye contact with Annalisa. "All clear. Doctor's orders, you're going inside to rest on a comfy couch in a room with a fireplace. You have a choice of transport. I can carry you or two men will form a chair lift."

The dragon snarled and snapped huge teeth. *No other man touches her. Mine!*

The doctor tapped him on the shoulder and Murdoch gladly stepped back. Good timing. The older man wanted to speak to his patient and meanwhile, he needed to have a serious talk, hell, he needed to pound some sense into his off-the-rails dragon.

"If you don't mind," Annalisa said to the doctor, "I came all this way to deliver a message to Mr. Rudraige. I'd prefer he carry me to the couch."

Smug, the dragon settled down, curling his long tail around his short legs and oversized claws. Murdoch started when the damn beast actually heaved a contented sigh. *For crying out loud.*

He took a deep breath, stepped forward, and gave the medic a nod. "Doctor, if you'll supervise the extraction?"

"Good. First let me check her legs. They look unimpeded. Go slowly."

Annalisa slipped her arms around Murdoch's neck and he slid one arm under her knees. Then he lifted slowly and carefully. Not easy when his dragon realized what was happening and started prancing around like a total fool. As Murdoch stepped back and straightened, he realized they were in a circle of uniformed men.

"Thanks for your help," he said quietly, "Now back to work." The guards scattered. "If you'll lead the way, Doctor. And open the front door. Inside, we're going left down the hall to the library."

The physician set a slow stately pace. Which gave

Murdoch time to enjoy the feel of Annalisa in his arms. Her hair tickled his neck. The gentle fragrance of shampoo filled his nostrils. It would have been a wonderful interlude if it hadn't been for his dragon. Not satisfied with Murdoch carrying the woman, the beast offered vivid suggestions for her immediate seduction.

Stop right now, he mentally shouted at the dragon, *or I swear, I'll drop her.*

Horrified, the dragon froze. The graphic mental images of kissing and undressing Annalisa, of claiming her with rough sex on top of his hoard disappeared.

Chapter Four

Breathing in the salt-laden night air, Annalisa resisted nuzzling her face into Murphy's neck. He had facial hair, too long to be scruff but very short and carefully trimmed for a beard. She discovered an almost uncontrollable desire to stroke it. Were the whiskers soft or bristly?

He was tall, well over six feet, with broad shoulders and a chest of solid muscles that flexed when he walked. She certainly wasn't a lightweight yet he'd lifted her with ease and strolled across the gravel driveway like she weighed nothing. The man wasn't even breathing hard. He must work out a lot.

Wearing dress pants and a light blue shirt with the sleeves rolled up, his tie was gone, and the open top button revealed the smooth tanned skin of his neck. What a coincidence, he looked like a business executive just home from the office before he changed into casual clothes.

Or, Annalisa's inner critic snarked, *like a billionaire*

pissed that an employee just ruined his front gate. Should she apologize again?

No, she was here, at her own expense, to alert Murphy to a critical Muirdris issue. She should, however, as an employee, stop her silent litany of his sexy attributes. She was damn grateful that Muirdris HR's anti-sexual harassment policy didn't include private thoughts.

Where was her phone? Raising her head, Annalisa said, "My bag. I need my bag from the car."

Without missing a step, Murphy said, "Doctor, please use the house intercom right inside the door to call the gate. Tell one of the sentries to bring all of Annalisa's belongings from the car into the library."

His voice rumbled through his chest, and the vibration against her body sent a shiver of awareness through her. Which she ignored. "Thank you," she murmured.

"No problem," he said, his breath ruffling a strand of her hair. Inside, they crossed over a foyer floor of blue and white marble squares. A massive crystal chandelier hung from the ceiling. What? No frescos?

Murphy carried her past a sweeping staircase and turned down the carpeted hall. To her amazement, the library really was cozy. After the foyer and a glimpse of the massive living room with an expanse of glass wall overlooking the ocean, she was expecting something rivaling Beauty and the Beast's book room. This space did have two walls of floor to ceiling shelves, but the overall size was more Long Beach middle class than Boston billionaire. The wood burning fireplace appeared almost rustic.

Murphy set her gently down at one end of a cushioned sofa, her feet up and her back propped against the armrest. The doctor placed his black bag beside the sofa, pulled out his little light thingy and checked her pupils.

"How's your head?" he asked, "Your neck?"

"Achy, not pain. My chin is sore."

"There's a laceration there from the airbag. Also you have a bruise forming on the edge of your eyebrow. Were you wearing glasses?"

Mr. Rudraige looked over the doctor's shoulder, his handsome face furrowed with concern.

"Yes," she said. "I did have on sunglasses."

The physician nodded and rattled off a list of head, neck and vision symptoms. "I don't think you have a concussion, but if you experience any of those signs, call me immediately."

"My phone…"

"Your purse is coming," the doctor said, "Now,

let's get started cleaning and bandaging those cuts and checking the bruises."

"Doctor," she said, grasping his hand and giving it a little squeeze. "Please don't think I'm ungrateful, but there's something extremely important I must tell Mr. Rudraige before you patch me up. Seriously, I couldn't relax until he's made aware of what's going on and he has examined the evidence I brought."

"All right." The doctor looked like he wanted to protest. Instead, he gave her a brief nod. "I'll step down the hall, check in with my daughter. Send me word when your business is finished."

"I will and thank you again."

When the doctor opened the library door, Ryan, the only gate guard whose name she remembered, was there. "Hey Doc, I brought your container of bandages and antiseptics." He offered a plastic bin.

"Thanks Ryan, could you put it by my bag over there?"

"Sure," Ryan said, coming into the room. She craned her neck to see her oversized purse dangling from one of his wrists.

"Thank goodness," she murmured, relief pouring through her.

Cradled in Ryan's other arm was her suitcase stuffed inside a large trash can. The corners of her case above the rim of the can looked like they'd been flattened by a steamroller. The zipper gaped open, and bits of her clothing protruded.

Murphy, um…Mr. Rudraige raised a questioning eyebrow at the trash can, then up to the man holding it.

Ryan handed over her purse, delivered the bandages, then he faced their boss and squared his shoulders. "The suitcase is heavily damaged, sir, and leaking a white fluid and something pink—shampoo or lotion—I estimate at least two containers of liquid are broken." He met Mr. Rudraige's disapproving look. "It was this or a big garbage bag, sir."

Annalisa rummaged for her phone, anxious to show Mr. Rudraige the pictures of the emails. "Quick thinking, Ryan," she murmured. "Thank you. I'd be mortified if anything spilled on Murphy's carpet."

She noticed Ryan's eyebrow arching. *Oh shit.* She was brainwashed by the Muirdris tradition of using first names.

With a little shrug, Mr. Rudraige said, "Good decision, Ryan. Please take the whole mess to the kitchen. We'll hope Ms. Bridget can salvage something from Annalisa's clothing."

What? Wait. "Is Bridget your cook? A maid?" Why should his servants clean up her suitcase and clothing? She could manage. Before she could call Ryan back, the door closed behind him.

"Bridget is a temporary housekeeper. She'll be here soon."

"Oh." She'd check with Bridget after her talk with the boss. Opening her phone, she scrolled to the photos of the emails. Mr. Rudraige was pacing. "Please sit down," she said, "your hovering is making me nervous."

He perched on the edge of the coffee table in front of her. Hands clasped, he rested his elbows on his knees. "Is this really so important you need to tell me before you get medical attention?"

"Absolutely." She began by describing her reactions this morning when she'd opened the emails—only hours ago? She stressed the deadline then handed over her phone, and he read the emails and the attachment carefully.

By the time she'd finished talking and he'd studied the attachments, she was exhausted. His face was a thundercloud.

"Ms. Bartello, Muirdris Shipping and I owe you a huge debt of gratitude. If anyone else had shown me these, I would have thought was a joke. But considering all the trouble you went through to bring me this, and what's happened since you got here, I know these have to be real."

She stared at him. True, she'd considered a prank at first, but it never occurred to her that the president of Muirdris might not believe the emails.

"Do you have any idea who the sender, the conspirator, might be?"

"No clue," he said shaking his head. Her heart sank.

He went on, "I'm hoping someone can trace back these messages."

"Me too," she agreed. "Who will you ask to do that?"

"You want to know who I trust?"

"Exactly." She studied him, especially his hazel green eyes.

"If you'd asked that same question at lunchtime today, I would have said I trust every employee at Muirdris. Especially the managers and directors because I know each of them personally."

Her gaze dropped to her phone. "The stakes are so high, it's not so easy for me to trust. After I couldn't get through to Finnian, he went back on my suspect list."

Murphy…uh Mr. Rudraige stiffened, and his eyes grew round.

She waved a hand. "I don't honestly think he's

selling Muirdris protocols, but when you consider everything that's at risk here. This is so important, Murphy." She lowered her voice. "This could destroy your company."

"I know." He dropped his head to his hands. "We need to recruit reliable help. Figure out who goes on our short list, keep it to a really select group, and all start digging."

She gave her head a little shake. "If we don't figure out who the bad guy is, if the leak isn't stopped right away, this could be just the beginning."

"Have you told anyone else?"

"Not a living soul. My best friend Liz knows I'm here in Boston on Muirdris business, but she has no inkling what that business is. Both HR and Finnian think I'm on personal leave."

"What prompted you to go looking for Victoria in Boston?"

She'd already told him about her adventures in the corporate office but didn't think Victoria answering the support line on a Saturday was relevant. Hearing the story now, he chuckled.

"Nobody's assistant would let me anywhere near," she explained, "because I refused to say why I was asking." Her arm itched. When she lifted a hand to scratch, Mr. Rudraige gently grabbed her wrist.

"Let me see."

She pointed to a bloody gash above her elbow.

"I believe," he said, "there could be a sliver of glass in there. You need to let the doctor check you over, clean those out. Then we'll talk more."

She surprised herself by turning her hand over and fitting it into his. A flash of heat ran through her body. *Stop that.* She had more important issues ping-ponging around in her brain. What was he going to do while she was getting patched up? Sure, it was the man's company, not hers, but she had a vested interest both as an employee and now as a whistleblower. She curled her lip. *Heroine sounded much better.*

Her hand jerked in his.

"What's wrong?" he asked.

"Ugly thought. Do you honestly think that truck was trying to break through your gate? Or were they out to eliminate me? Squash me like a bug?"

"We can't know for sure." His grip on her hand tightened. "I'll admit, I'm concerned they might've been after you. That's why I asked who knew you were coming here to see me and why."

She shivered. "What about reporting to the local police?"

"Already done, by Ryan, my head of security. I'm going to try to keep your name off the official report."

"Thanks."

"Then with your permission, I can also handle the rental car company."

"You personally?"

"I'm sure Ryan thinks he can be more impartial. We'll also get my insurance company involved." He leaned forward. Her breath caught in her throat. Was he going to take her in his arms?

A knock on the door jerked him back. "Come —"

"One minute," she called out louder. Grabbing his hand in both of hers, Annalisa held it, and met his gaze with a steely one of her own. "Do something for me."

"What?"

"Wait for me."

"Pardon?"

"While I'm getting patched up, please don't talk to anyone about the emails. Be thinking of who to call, make a list, but I want us to discuss the names before you decide. Will you do that for me?"

"I will, Annalisa, but you make it sound like you don't trust me to handle this. I've been uh, running this company for many years. My instincts are good, my judgement is excellent. It's disappointing to find out you don't have more confidence in me."

"That's not the way I meant it. I have loads of confidence in you." She mentally crossed her fingers as she lied. "It's only natural for me to want to be involved, at least for a little while. Don't you agree? Considering all the expense, trouble, and even danger I went through to get to you?"

He frowned at her.

"Go ahead and let the doctor in," she said.

Chapter Five

Murdoch sat upright and tense in the leather chair behind a small writing desk in his first-floor office. Right down the hall from the library…and Annalisa. The intriguing employee from California who travelled all the way across the country to warn him—well, to warn his brother—and yet didn't trust him.

The intercom on the desk buzzed.

"Yes?"

"It's Ryan. We've got the front gate security video ready for you to view."

"Excellent. You were working the change of shift at the gate when Annalisa pulled up, right?"

"Yes, sir."

"Transfer a copy of the video to the computer in my small office, and then join me here. We'll review it together and you can describe what happened."

"On my way."

Minutes later, Ryan pulled up a chair beside him and Murdoch said, "As soon as the police see the video, I'm hoping they'll declare the collision a hit and run and make an all-out push to find the truck. Meanwhile, let's do our best to keep Annalisa's name out of it."

"Umm, Murdoch?"

"What?"

"If you make a big deal to enough people about covering up Annalisa's name, it's bound to cause talk. After we view this and share it with our local police, let me deal with the rental car company, their insurance company and ours. If I let them come to the conclusion that the truck was targeting you, it changes everything. They'll buffer you. Also, they move slow."

"Okay, I see your point." *Exactly what he'd already planned to do.* "You handle it, Ryan, and thanks."

"One other thing…" His security chief all but squirmed in his chair.

"Spit it out, Ryan."

"All right, *Murdoch*. Do you want me to alert the rest of the team to call you Murphy? Otherwise it'll have to be *sir*. And we know how you love being called sir."

"Let's get through tonight." *Last thing I want to do is undermine what little trust she has in me.* "I'll correct Annalisa's misunderstanding first thing in the morning and we can all go back to Murdoch."

"Shall I warn Ms. Bridget when she gets here or will you, sir?"

"*Damn it to hell.*" His hands curled into tight fists. "I keep forgetting I invited that busybody housekeeper into my house. Would she remember to call me Mr. Rudraige?"

"Not without reminders which will lead to a million questions. The woman is a born snoop. When she subbed at the Estate, their head of security discovered her going through a closet drawer of Murphy's boxer briefs."

"Why the hell didn't somebody warn me?"

"As you said, you only have to make it through tonight. My money's on Annalisa being up and around by breakfast. If *she* decides she doesn't want Bridget in the house, what can you do but send the housekeeper on her way?"

He grumbled and said, "Show me the crash."

Murdoch discovered he and his dragon could barely watch the video once. When the monitor showed the truck backing away, leaving Annalisa trapped in her crumpled car, he jumped to his feet.

"Enough." Stomach knotted, jaw clenched, Murdoch had to get to Annalisa. "Ryan, go make your calls. Be sure to waylay Ms. Bridget. I need to find out what's taking the doctor so long." Translation: he needed to hurry the doctor on his way.

The dragon rampaged. Roaring, his claws raked an imaginary foe. They had to go to her. Now. See for themselves that she was all right. If reassurance didn't come pretty damn soon? The beast promised he'd take charge, track down the truck driver and tear his head off.

Murdoch burst into the library to find Annalisa alone and dozing on the couch. His heart lurched in his chest. God, she was beautiful. The shallow scratch on her chin was still red and he longed to kiss it. Her eyes blinked opened, she smiled and whispered, "Hello."

"How are you feeling?" He slid to his knees beside the couch and tenderly grasped one of her hands. Seeing her pinky finger was bandaged, he winced.

"All better." She wiggled her fingers. "Seriously, I'm terrific. Help me sit up?"

He shot to his feet, lifted her off the couch, cradled her against his chest. "Did the doctor okay this?"

"Sitting," she insisted.

He set her back down so her feet touched the floor.

"Thanks Murphy." Annalisa grinned. "You took the long way around, but it worked."

He sat across from her on the coffee table. Every

time she called him Murphy, his dragon growled. *I'll tell her tomorrow, she'd been through enough today*, he promised the beast.

Still, she was already recovering nicely. Maybe he was secretly afraid to tell her. Afraid that her already shaky confidence in him would evaporate entirely the minute she found out he wasn't the high and mighty, all powerful Murphy.

She'll love us, his dragon insisted.

Yeah, right. More fairy tales.

He leaned closer. "Are you hungry? Do you need something for pain?"

"I'm not in pain and I'd rather eat when you do. Let's finish discussing our plan to uncover who sent the emails. Did you come up with a list?"

"Sort of. Knowing it's best to keep our circle small, the first person I thought of is Gahaji. He's the head of Muirdris's worldwide security and—"

"Wait. Gahaji? That's an unusual name. Do his friends shorten it?"

"I call him Ji."

"Oh god, Ji works for you?" She bit her bottom lip. "I forgot to tell you about…that's the name Darren mentioned when I overheard him discussing the details of the secret project Finnian put me on."

"Sounds like good news. If Darren was talking to

Ji, that alone could clear Vic's assistant."

The intercom buzzed. Murdoch looked up and said, "Open line."

A familiar voice filled the room. "Sir, it's Ryan. Ms. Bridget is here and wants to know if Annalisa would like something to eat? Maybe a bowl of soup?"

"Or a real dinner?" Murdoch whispered to her with his best puppy-dog expression. Now that he knew Annalisa was safe and healing, he realized how hungry he was.

She smiled at him and her stomach rumbled. "Ryan? Please thank Ms. Bridget and tell her the doctor cleared me for all foods. Since Mr. Rudraige and I are starving, we'd appreciate whatever and as much as she can rustle up."

Ryan stifled a snort through the intercom, turning it into a slight cough. "Oh, and sir, I also have a message for *you*."

Annalisa's head went up, like she'd scented something in the wind.

He couldn't sense anything out of the ordinary, so he continued to refine the dinner plans. "Ryan, could you help Ms. Bridget by setting up dinner in the conservatory?"

"Yes, sir. Um, about the message—"

"We'll have coffee and dessert on the ocean side

terrace. Ask somebody to light the lanterns and turn on the heaters up there."

"Will do," Ryan said. "Sir, could you meet me in the hall to—"

"Ryan?" Annalisa said, "I can't stand the suspense a moment longer. You'd better tell Murphy who his message is from."

"What message is that?" Murdoch asked.

"The chief of police," Ryan sounded defeated. "Left you a *private* message about, you know, the crash."

"Private? It's my crash," Annalisa pointed out. "I'd like to hear what the police have to say,"

"Ryan," Murdoch said, "Was that Chief O'Malley who called?"

Ryan heaved a long, loud, exasperated sigh.

A lightbulb went off over Murdoch's thick skull. "Oh, a *private* message. Never mind, Ryan, I'll meet you in the hall."

Chapter Six

Annalisa stood and followed hot on Murphy's heels as far as the library door. When he stopped at the closed door, and frowned back at her, she fisted her hands on her hips.

"I'm coming, too," she insisted.

He shook his head. "You should be resting. Besides, I'd rather—"

She went up on tiptoe, glared at him. "Look Mr. Rudraige, I deserve to hear whatever the chief has to say about *my accident*. Don't you dare treat me like some fainting female. Whatever it is, I can take it. I am not a wimp. No secrets."

She caught Murphy's wince. After a moment, he opened the door.

"You may as well come in, Ryan. Annalisa insists on hearing the police report."

Leading the way carefully back the couch, she slowly let out a long breath and gingerly sank down in her corner. She'd gotten up too quickly. That, combined with losing her temper and lack of food, made her woozy. A fact she'd keep hidden from Murphy Rudraige, no matter what it took.

Ryan and Mr. Rudraige sat in the twin overstuffed chairs across the coffee table from her sofa. Then the boss gave Ryan a brief, encouraging nod to proceed.

Clearing his throat, Ryan said, "After reviewing our security video, it's Chief O'Malley's professional opinion that the crash was no accident."

"Right..." *Any fool could figure out that much.* Annalisa shot Ryan a ghost of a smile, mentally urging him to skip to the bottom line.

"From the video," Ryan plodded on, "the police were able to get a profile shot of the person behind the wheel. They're currently accessing multiple databases, trying to identify the driver. At the same time, the partial plate number they pulled from the video, led them to a stolen vehicle report filed earlier today. The local police have issued a multi-state bulletin to be on the lookout for the truck."

That was it? Annalisa tilted her head and stared at Ryan. "Thanks for the update. But none of that is earthshattering or scary. What did the Chief of Police say that you wanted to tell Murphy and keep from me?"

Several emotions flashed across Ryan's face. Was that last one admiration? It vanished too quickly to be sure. She darted a glance at Mr. Rudraige. He looked like he wanted to wring someone's neck. Hers?

With no direct order from Mr. Rudraige, Ryan finally hunched his shoulder and said, "The chief is convinced the driver of the truck was trying to kill you. His message to Mr. Rudraige was, *"until we apprehend the driver of that truck, Ms. Bartello needs to watch her back."*

"Thank you for—" she began, grateful to Ryan for not holding back.

"That's enough," Mr. Rudraige growled, shooting to his feet. "Ryan, call my brother's house. Borrow as many of his security team as you can get. Then I want you to—"

"Wait, Murphy," Annalisa said in a low voice as she walked around the coffee table and placed a gentle hand on his arm. "Before you call out the National Guard and turn this beautiful home into a real fortress, could we discuss this?"

"There's nothing to discuss." He sounded pissed, but he didn't pull his arm away. "If it takes a fortress, then that's what—"

"I was going to suggest," she interrupted, "to help

us decide who to confide in, you and I go to the head-quarters building in Boston. I've found looking people in the eye, watching their faces, helps me to evaluate them. Don't you agree?"

His brows lowered. "Too dangerous."

"Is there any other way to accomplish the same goal?"

"Maybe." A moment later, he covered her hand with one of his own. "I have a top of the line telecom-munications system in a room downstairs. How about you and I agree on two or three candidates. Then we'll arrange to interview each of them from here via satel-lite link. You can study their faces while I ask a few pertinent questions. Then we'll choose, confide in our number one choice, and get her or him busy tracking down the sender of the emails."

He fiddled with something in his pocket. "With a bit of luck, perhaps our person can think of a plan to give us more time. I'd like to set a trap for the spy and nail him."

"That's an excellent plan. Except when it comes down to you and I executing that last part. Traps can be complicated to pull off and we aren't detectives."

"Good point," Mr. Rudraige agreed. "But if the person we choose is talented with computers and net-works, they'll do the ground work. We won't actually arrest anyone, just identify the traitor, ensure we've gathered enough evidence, and turn everything over to the authorities."

"Does a talented someone come to mind?"

"I'd like us to interview Ji. See if you agree that he's a man to be trusted. Also, Vic, you know her as Victoria. Before we speak to either one of them, I want to try to contact Devlin."

"One of your directors?"

"Yes. You know this is very much a family company and most of the directors are my cousins. Besides being a relative, Devlin's amazing with computers."

"Same rules apply, even though he's family?" she asked. "You talk to him while I study his face?"

"Absolutely."

Ryan's phone buzzed. "May I?" Ryan asked, pulling the phone from his pocket. "Ah, dinner's ready. Why don't I bring it downstairs? You can eat while you wait for Devlin's call."

She looked up to study Murphy's face. "After we're done, we could still have coffee and desert out on your terrace."

"Nice thought." A slow smile spread across his handsome face. "A very nice thought." He turned. "Thank you, Ryan. Please arrange transport for our food to the secure room downstairs, while I escort Annalisa to the guest room." He faced her again.

He snagged her over-sized purse and they moved down the wide hallway together, past several closed doors. At the open door, he handed over her purse, and gestured into the room. "Make yourself at home."

Just what a corporate president says to his employee. This was getting complicated.

"I'm serious, Annalisa." His face was expressionless. "Help yourself, to anything you find. You can shower, the hairbrushes, toothbrushes are all new. You'll find an assortment of sweats, jeans, and sweaters in the closet. Meanwhile, I'll get a message to Devlin in Japan, get him on the secure line. And I'll put Ji and Vic on alert, tell them to expect my call."

She peeked through the open door. The room was gigantic, decorated like a museum. The total opposite of the cozy library. With a shiver, she tried to joke, "Will you leave a trail of breadcrumbs for me to find you?"

"I'll be waiting right here, outside your door."

A wave of warmth enveloped her. Followed by a chorus of *he's the boss, he's the boss, don't even think about it.* The warning chanted at full volume through her brain until the gray cells turned to mush.

She showered and shampooed at warp speed. After drying with the world's softest towel, she hurried to the walk-in closet in search of anything that would fit her curves.

One step inside and Annalisa gasped. *The damn closet was the same square footage as her living room.* Dazed, she forgot to hurry. There were freaking aisles of rods, racks and shelves. Crystal chandeliers glittered over multiple free-standing islands, a door opened into a 365-degree mirrored alcove. There was a cool room, a shoe wall, a jewelry wall and a walk-in safe.

The designer jeans were marked her size but a snug fit. A thin silk tank top was an excellent substitute for a bra and over it she pulled on a cashmere sweater.

When it was time to tame her thick curly hair, she could no longer ignore the obviously expensive bedroom furniture and ritzy décor. Plugging in the blow dryer behind the bedside table, Annalisa sat on the edge of the four-poster bed, and dried her hair while she gawked.

When she was finally ready and opened the door, Murphy, uh, Mr. Rudraige was waiting. Just like he'd promised.

"Hungry?" he asked.

"Lead the way," she said with a grin.

The spiral stone stairs down to the secure room was like something out of Hogwarts. While the inside of the sleek room reminded her of mission control.

Dinner consisted of several different dishes, like a gourmet buffet. A mouthwatering selection. After they finished, he stacked the dishes out of sight and returned to stand beside her.

"Devlin hasn't returned my call yet," he said. "His assistant said he's on one of our container carriers headed out to sea."

"That's a shame. You can't contact him on your vessel?"

"Well…I could, however, I'm not as happy with the security and the reception can be less than great. And now time's running out. Let's move on. Victoria or Ji first?"

"Vic," she said and smiled. "Then Ji."

"Can you see the screen okay from here?"

"Sure. Are you going somewhere?"

"I'll be right there, at the console." He indicated the control panel in the center of the room. "I'd prefer not to put you in the spotlight. Unless you—"

"I'm fine right here." She took in a calming breath. "Let's talk to Vic."

Once she got over the sheer perfection of Victoria's figure, her face, and that hair—damn, the Muirdris vice president looked more like a top model—Annalisa could study her facial expressions, her hand movements and body language. Watched her lips and eyes as she answered questions. The woman appeared curious, and slightly amused. Then she seemed to pick up on Mr. Rudraige's nerves.

"What's wrong?" Vic asked, her brows drawing together.

Mr. Rudraige slid a glance over to Annalisa, she gave him a slight nod, and whispered, "Enough."

"That's all for now, Vic. Please stand by for fifteen minutes. Out." He tapped the keyboard in front of him. The wall screen went dark.

Without looking over to her, he said, "Ready for Ji?"

"Yes."

Ji was a handsome young man with ebony skin and an infectious smile. After a bit of small talk, Mr. Rudraige asked an identical list of questions to Ji while she studied the security VP with the same sharp eye. *Very different personalities.* And Ji caught on to Mr. Rudraige's nervousness faster than Vic had. And he was more aggressive questioning his boss.

"If there's trouble, anything going on," Ji insisted,

"you need to tell me, Mur—"

Ji's audio cut off, his image jiggled. Annalisa leaned forward. Ji was on his feet, his lips moving, "What the hell?"

The screen went dark.

Chapter Seven

Murdoch grabbed his cell phone from its charger beside the keyboard. Before he could access the contact list, the instrument chimed with an incoming call. He tapped to accept and turned on the speaker. "Victoria?" he barked. "What's happening?"

"An explosion. That's all I know, Murdoch. There's been an explosion. Below. On the lobby level or underground parking structure. Whole building is evacuating now."

"Okay, get out." His phone beeped with another call. He ignored it. "Vic, can you stay on the line with me while you go down the stairs? It's important."

"Certainly," Vic said. "Do you need me to stay here? In the secure room?"

"Hell, no. Get moving. Nothing's more important than your life."

During the faint background scuffling sounds, he beckoned Annalisa to join him at the long table. When she slid into the chair beside him, he whispered, "I want to trust her, especially now that the headquarters has been attacked. What's your vote?"

"I vote yes. Both your executives seemed trustworthy. She scored a slight edge based on staying calm in a crisis."

He nodded. He'd always regarded foxes as nervous creatures, until he'd met Victoria. "Nerves of steel," he whispered to Annalisa.

The piercing wail of a siren erupted from the phone's speaker. "Whoa." He hurried to lower the volume.

"Sorry," Vic shouted over the din, "We know the evacuation siren works. Hang on. I'm in the hall; will be taking the back stairs."

After a few minutes, the shriek of the siren became background noise. "Whew," Vic blew out a breath. "All right, I'm headed down the stairwell. Tell me what's up with you."

She had a lot of stairs to go, so Murdoch started at the beginning, with Annalisa receiving the first email in Long Beach. He went through the rest of her day today, the trip to Massachusetts, and the truck rear-ending Annalisa's rental car in his driveway. And finished with their decision to ask Vic to set up a blind contact to the person offering to sell corporate secrets. Then convince that person to give them more time to pay.

"Well, hell," Vic muttered. "When, exactly, is the payoff due?"

"Five minutes before midnight—"

"What?" Vic shrieked.

"Pacific time," he blurted out.

"Way to scare the living crap out of me." She took a deep breath. "All right, I accept the challenge. On my way out, I'll get an update on the situation here. Maybe a car in the garage exploded from natural causes. Anyway, let's assume structural engineers will close the building for inspections. Say forty-eight hours. Maybe more. I'll need to do my email responding and negotiating from my personal secure location."

"I can't tell you," he said, "how delighted I am that you pressured me...um... *talked me* into that expenditure last year."

"I'll save the *told-you-so* until after we've caught this slime-ball."

"Victoria, I'm on my cell and anxious to get back on a secured phone. Contact us in my downstairs room the minute you're locked down. Annalisa will share her California office computer password, so you can get into her email in Long Beach, and start tracing the source from the original messages."

"Annalisa?" Victoria asked. "The name sounds famil—"

"Hi Victoria," Annalisa spoke for the first time. "How's my favorite IT support tech?"

"It *is* you. When things calm down, we'll chat."

"Deal," Annalisa said.

"Ladies…" Murdoch said.

"Hold on," Vic said in a harsh whisper. "Someone's coming *up* the stairs."

"Be careful," he warned.

"Brian, you scared me." Vic sounded very much in control. "Are there any injuries?"

"None," the Muirdris building supervisor said in a tight voice. "Automobile exploded in the parking garage, no injuries and no witnesses. The big question is, was it a bomb? Either way, the timing's in our favor. The building is practically empty. I'm going up, checking floor by floor, until the firefighters catch me, throw me out."

"Structural damage?"

"I'm certain, when Murdoch does get back to me, he'll insist on a complete inspection."

"Bet you hear from him any minute."

"And *that* timing," Brian said, lowering his voice, "is definitely crap." Murdoch tilted his head to hear the supervisor. "Why the hell was Murphy called away so abruptly today?"

"You think there's a connection?"

"Hell if I know. I'll admit, working with Murdoch isn't my first choice. If Murphy was stateside, he'd be here on site by now. Or well on his way."

Victoria laughed. "I'm sure Murphy appreciates your loyalty. But whichever one rushed here, Murdoch or Murphy, he'd end up standing across the street, behind the barricades, just like you will when the first responders find you in here. Hurry up, Brian, do what you need to do, then get out. I'm evacuating now."

A moment later, Vic said into her phone, "Call Brian. I'm signing off. Back in forty-five minutes." And she disconnected.

Murdoch mentally reviewed the conversation and cringed. Vic had called him Murdoch, more than once. Annalisa was an intelligent woman. While it was way too soon to reveal his second nature as a sea dragon, the twin thing was out of the bag. He needed to clear up the mistaken identity. He'd better start talking, groveling, fast.

"I'm sure it's occurred to you," Annalisa said in a tight voice, "that the emails and the explosion might not be connected."

"Agreed. Unless Muirdris gets a blackmail demand or another threat, the explosion goes to the Boston police and Ji to deal with. We need Victoria working on the emails, and they should be our focus. We need her to get us more time."

She stood, slung her bag over one shoulder and gave him a steely look. "You promised me dessert. Something about a terrace with an ocean view?"

"Let me call ahead." He pressed the house intercom. Waiting for a response, he tried distracting her. "I'm counting on a big slice of warm cherry pie smothered in vanilla ice cream to soften you up for my abject apology."

She ignored him.

On the terrace, the pie waited in a small warmer beside a frosty container of home-made ice cream. He settled a silent Annalisa on the double lounger, bundled her in a thick blanket and served the dessert.

After the second bite, the cherry pie sat like a boulder in his stomach. He needed to apologize, now, for misleading her. Worse than that. For lying about his identity.

She slid her plate of untouched pie onto the side table and angled herself toward him.

Now was his chance. "I'm sorry abou—"

"I thought I could—" she started. They both

stopped abruptly.

"You go first," he said, the model of chivalry. "Remember, I said I'm sorry."

"You've been nice about so many things," she said, "I thought I could move past the fact that you've flat-out lied to me from the get-go. Totally misrepresented who you are."

His heart shriveled in his chest. The dragon hung his head.

"I tried," she went on, "but, come to find out, I can't instantly forget or forgive your lies. I'm really angry, livid, and horribly disappointed."

"I really am sorry. I—it all happened so fast. No, that's just an excuse. I—"

"Who the hell are you?" she demanded. "You look just like his picture. You're identical twins? Murphy's twin brother?"

"Yes, the younger twin. Name's Murdoch."

And my crazy dragon believes you're my, his, our mate. If I don't fix this, the beast will never forgive me. "Can you ever forgive me? What can I do to make it up to you?"

"Is this your house?"

"Yes, it's mine. You passed the turn off for Murphy's estate miles back. He lives closer to the city."

"Damn it. We need to repeat every conversation,

everything you've said to me, so I'll know which parts were lies." Her eyes shimmered, her hands clenched in her lap. "It's all been one big lie, ever since I got here, hasn't it?"

A tear escaped her eye and rolled down her cheek.

"Please…" He was terrified. Whatever he felt for this woman, it deserved the chance to grow. Or to die a natural death. It simply couldn't end this way.

"It hasn't," he murmured, "been one big intentional lie…no wait, I don't want to give you a list of feeble excuses. I admit I lied. I allowed the lie to continue. I regret that. Much more than you'll ever know. Could we start over? Like you said, we'll replay whatever conversations, on whatever subjects, you like? And from now on, you'll get nothing but the total truth from me?"

Her gaze dropped to her hands. "Let's hear one of the excuses."

"I was concerned about your injuries. When you assumed I was Murphy, I didn't want to correct you there and then."

"Well, that's right, you never introduced yourself as Murphy—"

"I should have told you I'm Murdoch."

"Talk like that isn't helping your case."

"The whole truth and nothing but," he said, swearing a solemn promise to Annalisa.

She frowned down to the watch on her wrist. His mind racing, he stopped, stared. And did a double take. The face of the watch was a cartoon. Cecil the sea serpent. It was a sign.

Fated mates, his dragon growled.

Murdoch's breath caught in his throat. Could the dragon be right? Was she his mate? After all this time, the one woman on Earth perfect for him? Er, *them?* His heart pounded as a tidal wave of hope flooded through him, filled him.

The dragon romped with excitement, flicking his long tail.

Start over. "Annalisa, I sincerely apologize for lying to you. Please allow me to show you how sorry I am by never lying again. I want us to be friends. And I more than understand if you need time to learn to trust me."

She gave him a slight, silent nod.

"Let me prove how much you mean to me."

Annalisa raised an eyebrow.

"As a friend," he amended and offered his hand. She returned the pressure and the handshake. Before she could withdraw, he dropped a kiss on her knuckles, released her and stood. "Let's have a do-over on the pie."

She ate quietly for a few bites, then began a conversation about building on cliffs. He stared into her expressive face. She was absolutely stunning. Long hair cascaded down her back, curling almost to her waist. It would look more magnificent wet, floating around her face, swaying with the ocean current.

She licked ice cream off her fork. He longed to lick the residue from her lips.

"It's especially dangerous," she said, "in Southern California."

"Dangerous," he muttered, no idea what he'd just agreed to.

"Because of all the landslides," she pointed out, "mud slides, and quakes."

He pulled himself together. "The bedrock here is very stable. And the view during the day is amazing. We could have coffee out here tomorrow morning, if you like; watch the sunrise."

"Sounds lovely. Especially if Victoria can convince the seller we're legit and buy us more time to make the deal."

"Ready to go back downstairs?"

"Yes."

Chapter Eight

Filling two travel-tumblers with fresh hot coffee, Annalisa brought them back to her place at the central table. Next to her, Murdoch accessed the computer, turned on his satellite phone, and made minor adjustments to the wall monitors.

"It could be a long night," she observed, sliding into the chair next to him. "Could you show me how to reset one of the clocks in the corner to California time? So I don't have to keep looking down at my watch?"

"Move your coffee a little to the left."

After she'd shifted her tumbler out of the way, he pressed a combination of keys on the keyboard, and a rectangle opened in the tabletop in front of her to reveal a wireless keyboard and mouse. "Slick."

He held up a finger. "Let me enable the system for dual control."

"Two players?" she teased, secretly warmed that he was so quick to allow her access.

"Exactly. Voice command is extremely distracting with more than one person in the room."

While they waited for Vic to join the conference, she covertly studied Murdoch. His long agile fingers danced over the keyboard. The man had great hands. As they moved, the muscles in his forearms flexed, mirroring. He glanced over, caught her staring, and shot her a sexy grin.

"Did you finish setting the clock?"

Oh, right. "Um—"

The computer chimed an alert. Vic's face appeared on the giant wall screen. Well, the top half of Victoria's face was visible over the monitor. Other equipment blinked and flashed behind her.

"Welcome back," Murdoch said. "Ready to hack into Annalisa's Long Beach computer?"

"I'll be gentle," Vic assured them. "What's the password?"

Proud of her security measures, Annalisa recited a gobbledygook combination of numbers, letters and symbols.

"Jeez," Murdoch muttered, "Paranoid?"

"Way to play it safe, Annalisa," Vic said, obviously impressed. "Okay, I'm in. Same password for the company email?"

"No," she said.

"Why am I not surprised?" Murdoch ribbed.

She rattled off an entirely different combination and added, "The emails in question are still in the in-box."

"I'm there." Vic narrowed her eyes at her screen. "Annalisa, you opened the attachment designated *sample* just one time?"

"Correct."

"Before I open it a second time and possibly trigger an auto-delete or some tracking reaction, I'm going to dig deeper. See where this puppy has travelled, maybe get back to where it originated. You two talk amongst yourselves. It'll take me a few minutes."

Without a word, Murdoch sat back, took a long drink of coffee. The silence gradually grew oppressive. Finally, Murdoch leaned close and whispered, "I like your watch. Are you a fan?"

She angled a skeptical look at him. He knew about Cecil the sea serpent? *Doubtful.* The man was simply making small talk, and she could prove it. "I am. You?"

"Absolutely. Cecil's a classic."

Proves nothing. Try this. "Which format did you like best?"

"Hard to choose," Murdoch said. "I enjoyed the puppet with his iconic voice, but the cartoon was great."

My god, he does know Cecil. "Where did you see the 1950 KTLA broadcasts? You weren't even alive in 1950."

He seemed to consider his answer. "The miracle of electronics," he said at last, "you can still watch episodes of *Time for Beany* on line."

"And the *Beany and Cecil* cartoon from 1988."

"Question," Vic said as her hair appeared over the top edge of her monitor. She straightened until her nose and eyes were visible.

"What?" Murdoch asked.

"Got what I need. And before I dig deeper into the dangerous territory of pinpointing the origin of this email, I'll use what I have so far. I can set up a safe way to reply. Is that right, Murdoch? You want me to reply with an offer to buy the Muirdris port protocols? Or I could try stalling by asking questions."

"No stalling. Offer to buy. Cautiously. We have to assume our seller knows something about the buyer. Impersonating him could prove dicey."

Annalisa said, "Based on the wording of the *deal one* email, I'd guess the seller doesn't know too much, other than a name and email address. Very likely Bartellino was a referral."

"That would be a comforting thought," Vic said,

typing fast. "Okay, I'm ready to bounce a reply."

"Wait." Murdoch said. "Before you press *send*, can you confirm we have an airtight backstory all set up?"

"Confirmed," Vic said. "I can personally vouch for the airtight part. I'm emailing the external details to you right now."

Murdoch added, "And an offshore account that'll look legit when—"

"Our account *is* legit," Vic insisted. "We're all set."

"Terrific. And finally, a drop site to receive the emailed protocols."

"Ready. And all set up to be easily and quickly connected to the seller and his financial assets."

"I apologize if I sound like I'm checking up on…"

"Any time," Vic assured him. "When we get into situations none of us have dealt with before, double checking is always a solid idea."

"Thanks for understanding," Murdoch muttered.

What was he referring to? Annalisa narrowed her eyes.

"If everyone is ready," Vic said, "let me send this."

"Go," he said.

"Send," she added, right behind him.

Vic blew out a shaky breath. "Done." Her voice sounded a tiny bit on edge. "Now let's brainstorm some delaying tactics we can use on our bad guy. While we're tracking him down."

"You can always demand assurances," Annalisa said, "Like a promise the data won't be sold elsewhere."

"Good," Vic said.

"How much time," Murdoch asked, "are you going to need to find him?"

Vic's eyebrows drew together. "I'm guessing about ten to twelve hours. Maybe longer. But I think we should stall to gain ourselves days not hours."

"No telling how long the reply from this first contact will take." Murdoch stood, stretched, and looked at Annalisa. "More coffee?"

She glanced back and forth between Vic and Murdoch. "We're staying up until we hear something—right?"

"That's the plan," Murdoch said. "Remember it could go right to the last minute. His deadline of midnight in Long Beach is three a.m. here."

"Then fill my tumbler, please," she said smiling. "I'm going to need the boost."

"You're already used to California time."

"Coffee."

Vic looked at them again. "Why don't you two find a couple of comfortable chairs and cat nap? I can signal you on the satellite phone the minute the email arrives."

In the library, the fire was dying. Only glowing embers remained on the grate. After Murdoch placed both his phones on the table beside the two coffees, he added logs and built up the fire. He turned to her, and hesitated, so she offered an encouraging smile and he joined her on the couch.

She slipped off her shoes and curled her bare feet under her.

Murdoch removed his shoes and extended his long legs, crossing his ankles. He spread his arm across the back of the couch.

"How about we go shopping tomorrow afternoon?" he offered.

"Into Boston?"

"Not that you don't look stunning in that outfit, but you could definitely use replacement clothing. We can grab a late lunch or early dinner. We could even check on the headquarters."

She smoothed the sleeve on the cashmere sweater. The fuzzy beauty easily cost more than a week of her salary. Right. Go shopping with the billionaire. All around embarrassing. Her most critical need was underwear. A jacket or coat would come in handy. But she seldom wore coats in California and she already had a lightweight rain jacket at home.

Murdoch scooted closer to her, placed a hand gently on her shoulder. "I can see the wheels turning. Here's the way I see it. You flew all the way across the country to warn us about a major threat to Muirdris. To start, I insist on reimbursing you for all your expenses, and that includes your airline ticket and rental car, as well as the smashed suitcase and ruined clothing as a result of being run down in my driveway."

She moved closer to Murdoch, touched his arm. "That's more than generous but until the —"

"Annalisa, no buts and no until's. I'd rather not lend you *my* clothes so no more arguments. Tomorrow, as soon as we get the protocol seller on the hook, and catch up on sleep, we'll do some clothes and grocery shopping."

"That's so generous and thoughtful." Without thinking, her fingertip sketched little circles on his shirt sleeve. She looked into his eyes and was enchanted. Her breathing sped up and her heart was pounding.

He leaned closer, lowered his voice for emphasis. "You make it damned easy to be thoughtful. The more

I'm with you, the more I find to admire."

She knew from the heat spreading up her neck and across her face she was turning red. "Me, too. That is, I can't get over how well you're managing one crisis after another. If it weren't for you handling everything, I'd be a basket case by now."

She started to duck her chin, to avoid his intense gaze. His index finger tucked under her chin and he gently lifted her head. "Don't hide your face. You're beautiful."

He dropped his glance to her lips and her mouth dried. *He was going to kiss her.* She inched closer until her knee met his thigh.

"If," he whispered, "I start anything you don't want, do anything you don't want me to do, just say no." His mouth hovered, almost touching hers. The heat from his breath caressed her lips. He smelled like the ocean and coffee. And something earthy she couldn't identify. He didn't move any closer.

She wanted this. Wanted to taste him. Feel his lips on hers. She ran her tongue along her parted lips. Still, he stayed frozen in place.

"Yes, please," Annalisa whispered at last.

Murdoch captured her mouth with his.

Chapter Nine

Murdoch struggled to keep his mouth gentle on Annalisa's lips. He wanted to feel her pressed against him. His fingers itched to explore, to roam over every inch of her luscious body. To caress her hair, stroke her skin, excite her, pleasure her. *Not yet.* Limiting his hands, he only allowed them to rest on her shoulders.

Control became more difficult as his senses rapidly filled with her. Like the intoxicating aroma of his soap and his shampoo, sharpened and enhanced by the heat of her body.

Annalisa opened her soft plump lips slightly. Like she was yielding, inviting him in. And that was a temptation he couldn't resist. He had to taste her. Murdoch ran his tongue along her bottom lip.

She moaned. The sound ignited him, sent molten desire exploding through his body. *Closer.* Lifting her hands, he guided her arms to circle around his neck and pulled her against him. *Deeper.* His mouth ravaged hers, his tongue questing into her mouth, teasing and tempting.

His dragon roared with joy, and this time Murdoch's human side listened. And whole heartedly agreed. *She is the one.* Annalisa was his fated mate. He still wasn't quite sure about all the ramifications of this discovery, but the fact of it was undeniable. His mate. They were destined to love each other, to be together through time. From this moment on, she became his primary goal. He would love, protect, and cherish Annalisa and their young.

Needing his mate closer still, Murdoch slid an arm under her legs and lifted her off the couch. Settling her on his lap, he hugged her. When she buried her face in his shoulder, he nuzzled her neck.

"Wait." Her head came up so fast it almost clipped his chin.

"What's wrong?"

"Let me up." She slipped her hands down, pressed her palms against his chest. Her legs scrambled to get off his lap.

"I will, I swear," he assured her and raised his hands as a sign of surrender. When she stopped squirming, he added, "Will you calm down and listen? For just a minute?"

Annalisa nodded and then angled her head to face him.

"After I've had my say," he explained, "if you still want to move, I'll help you up. But please let me say something first?" His mind raced. What could he say? What he needed was more time with her, a chance for Annalisa to get to know him, to fall in love with him.

He'd heard that very few humans believed in love at first sight. A higher number of them believed they had a soulmate, somewhere, but admitted they weren't sure how that worked. Well, neither did he.

No dragon in the Muirdris clan had found a mate, yet. Female dragons were few and far between and the one overture Murphy had made to a fire-breathing clan about possible mates had met with a flat rejection. The fire dragon's negative response had come after he learned that all the Muirdris sea dragons were the products of a generation of breeding between endangered sea serpents and dragons. The result—he and Murdoch and all their cousins—viewed themselves as the best of both species.

The fire breathers had begged to differ.

"Okay," Annalisa huffed. "What is it?"

"I didn't mean to rush you, if it felt that way to you, I apologize. I think we both agree, we need to talk. About this scary, horrible day, as well as the unexpected attraction between us. While we talk, I'd like us to stay just where we are. Honestly, Annalisa, it's been a hell of a day and having you close calms me."

Annalisa gave her butt a little wiggle and pressed against his hard cock. "You call that calm?" She met his gaze and gave him a giant eye-roll.

"No, that's definitely excitement and desire. You need to give credit for my body's *enthusiasm* to your hot kisses."

"So, no more kissing?"

"Not during our talk. Let's call a moratorium?"

She punched his arm and Murdoch's heart lifted. She couldn't be too angry if she could still tease him.

"It's a plan, then?" he asked. "We'll put a hold on those hot lips of yours while we snuggle and discuss. Cuddling with you feels amazingly tranquil after such a stressful day. Don't you agree?"

Her body relaxed. "Yes." Curling into him, she rested her head against his chest and let out a long sigh.

He heaved his own sigh, one of relief. *We're not out of the kelp beds yet,* he warned his dragon. *Slow, we need to go slowly.* The dragon snorted. **Show her the Hoard.**

This is not about riches, he started to explain and gave up.

"Even after such a frightening day," Annalisa whispered, "I'm still determined to see this through."

Wrapping his arms loosely around her, he gently stroked her back.

"Especially," she went on, "if there's any more I can do to help you catch the conspirator. I have three weeks of sick leave saved up. Not as much personal leave."

"After Vic makes contact," he said, "let's see if she changes her estimate on the time needed to locate our guy. Meanwhile, would you consider working your California job from here?"

"Here? Like in-your-house here?"

"Or at the downtown headquarters, if and when it's safe to go there. I can contact the head of Human Relations, have you reassigned."

She wrinkled her nose. "Working for you?"

Uh oh, he'd gone too far. "If you've been temporarily transferred here...uh, to Boston, that is, then you can choose any combination of reporting and working arrangements. Like you report to Vic, fulfill your California assignments in Boston or here at the house. And you and I will continue to work together on the locating the turncoat."

The satellite phone beeped. He reached around Annalisa and answered it.

"Hey, Vic. Should we go back downstairs?"

"Don't think that's necessary. This is a pretty simple update and good news. I've made contact, we have a confirmation email. There was no need for me to try stalling our target at this point. He's setting up a new off shore bank account and will have the wire transfer data for us in seventy-two hours. After payment, he's promising to send an encoded copy of the protocols."

"Three days?" he mused. "That should give you enough time to find the bastard."

"Exactly my plan. Meanwhile, I'll finish up our fictitious background and transfer lots of Muirdris money into an accessible bank account." Did he note a hint of teasing in her voice? He and his dragon winced at the mention of using clan-hoard as bait. "I'll keep you informed as I go," Vic said. "You two be careful."

"Thanks," he said, then couldn't help adding, "You be careful with my money."

"Always," Vic assured him. "What are your plans?

"After catching up on sleep, we'll concentrate on our truck driver and the explosion at HQ. See if there are *any* connections. You can send a signal to my cell if you need to talk to us in the secure room."

"Will do."

After the call was disconnected, Murdoch stood, bringing Annalisa with him. When she was steady on her feet, he pocketed both phones. "May I walk you to your room?"

"Thanks."

"Are we on for shopping tomorrow, or, I guess since it already is tomorrow, this afternoon?"

"I guess."

"You need replacement clothes, a new phone. And after you're set, we can check on the Muirdris headquarters building."

They walked side by side down the hallway. She half-turned to him and said, "The way you talked to Vic it sounded like we'd be staying here today, researching and looking for connections online."

"You're going to run out of clothes real fast." He pressed his lips closed, swallowing the suggestive remark that jumped into his mind about Annalisa forced to run around in the nude. Damn, as long as his feelings for her remained so one-sided, he needed to keep himself in check, keep his thoughts to himself. Coming on to her wouldn't help his cause.

"I'm figuring," he said, "we can do both. Find you enough outfits to last until the traitor is caught plus get an update on the Muirdris building. Then we can come back here for research."

"And what if the bomb in Boston was connected to my truck crash here? Isn't it dangerous for me to go back to the *scene of the crime*?"

"Maybe…" He though she was half-teasing, but his blood ran cold at the mental picture of his mate trapped under the rubble of the collapsed Muirdris offices. *New plan.* "How about we shop for clothes and a phone, then wait on visiting the building until the police and the bomb experts decide what's going on with the explosion?"

"I think *you* making an appearance at Muirdris is an excellent idea," she said.

Before she could expand on that thought, he vehemently shook his head. Standing in front of her closed bedroom door, she planted her feet, fisted her hands on her hips, and frowned at him.

"Stop shaking your head," she grumbled, "and hear me out. It doesn't matter if you're Murphy or Murdoch, your employees need to see you. Hear you say it'll be all right. They need to know you're talking with the police and the engineers. Don't you dare use me as an excuse not to go. I could stay nearby with Vic for an hour while you make an official appearance."

"You mean *leave* you?" he asked, over his dragon's furious screeches.

Her frown deepened. "Let me put it another way. If you're so deeply worried about my safety that you refuse to leave me with Vic for sixty minutes? That level of concern leads me to believe you know more about the situation than you've shared. That things are a hell of a lot worse, and I'm in more immediate danger, than you've been letting on. What are you keeping from me?"

Chapter Ten

As Annalisa had fallen asleep last night, she'd been dealing with an ugly combination of jetlag, whiplash, and inappropriate sexual attraction to her boss. And when she let her defenses down for more than an instant, fear stalked her, anxious to join the mix.

Annalisa woke at noon to discover that, thanks to the Tylenol she'd taken before sliding into bed and the hours of deep sleep, her two physical ailments had resolved. She propped two of the down pillows against the headboard and sat back to take stock. Her remaining issues? Fear and lust.

She could solve both concerns by flying home today. Get as far away from the truck driver and the bomber as possible. While putting serious distance between herself and Murdoch, the source of her sexual temptation.

Except, running away would mean she was a coward. It had taken courage to fly to Massachusetts, to sneak around the headquarters building, to drive to

Murdoch's mansion. She'd taken several brave steps to warn Muirdris. Now, she needed to stay, to help Vic and Murdoch figure out the identity of the conspirator. She needed to finish what she started, to see it through.

Was running away from Murdoch also a sign of cowardice? She shook her head. Different deal. Avoiding Murdoch could be a matter of survival. No matter how tempting, an affair with the owner of Muirdris would end up taking more from her than she could afford to lose. It would land her on the front page of the tabloids, as well as in the unemployment line. She'd be disgraced and notorious. And she'd very likely lose her heart in the process.

There was a soft tap on the door. "Ms. Bartello?" a woman's voice asked.

"I'm awake, come in."

The door opened just wide enough to let in a short woman with curly white hair and sharp blue eyes. "I'm Bridget, the substitute housekeeper. Can I get you anything? Would you like breakfast in bed?"

"The breakfast part sounds wonderful, Bridget, but I'd rather not eat alone. Is Murdoch up?"

The housekeeper took two steps further into the room, stopped, and folded her hands at her waist. "He's been up for nearly two hours, what with talking on the phone and messing about with that little computer. And then he went for a swim. Said he'd wait to eat with you." She punctuated the end of her summary with a loud sniff. Disapproval of the master eating with the house guest?

Annalisa gave the housekeeper a smug smile. "When you see Murdoch, tell him I'll join him for breakfast in half an hour."

"All right."

She bit her bottom lip. Unless she wanted to spend hours searching, she'd better get off her high horse and ask for directions to the food. "Is the dining room on this floor?"

"Yes," Bridget said. "On the other side of the living room."

"Thank you." The minute the door closed behind Bridget, Annalisa threw back the covers and scrambled out of bed. She was pawing through a stack of folded jeans in the humungous closet when it hit her. *A swim? In January?*

The lack of personal clothing, her own hair products, and cosmetics cut her usual mirror-time in half. She stuck her tongue out at her reflection, checked her Cecil watch, and hurried to find the dining room.

Murdoch waited just inside the door. Claiming one of her hands, he dropped a kiss on her cheek and took a step back. She considered complaining but his smile took her breath away. Dressed in a blue silk shirt and slacks, he looked like a stock photo model for "rich playboy at home."

She managed to stifle her laugh, but humor lifted her lips in a smile.

"Hungry?" he asked as he led her to the head of a long, polished table. *Wow*. She counted twelve matching chairs with extras parked along the walls.

"Starving," she confided. The two china place settings sparkled, the silver coffee service in front of her place glowed in the indirect sunlight from the long windows behind her chair.

"If you'll pour us both coffees, I'll load up the plates." He took their plates and crossed the room to the buffet. "Eggs?"

"Please."

"How do you like them cooked?"

"Scrambled is fine. I could serve mysel—"

"I know," he said over his shoulder, "But I'm having fun here, learning more about you. Bacon, ham, or sausage? Or all three?"

"Is it link sausage or patties?"

"Both."

"I should have known," she muttered under her

breath. "One link sausage and two strips of crisp bacon, please."

She was on her second cup of coffee by the time Murdoch placed the piled-high plate of food in front of her. "Thank you." And set down a matching one for himself.

"Now," she said, waving a bacon strip, "ease my conscience and tell me there's an orphanage nearby you donate all the extra food to. Or that someone here will eat all the leftovers."

"Guaranteed," he said. "The security staff loves all types of breakfast food and with three shifts, they'll eat it anytime, day or night."

"I heard you took a swim earlier. Does this place have an indoor pool?"

He raised his brows. "How did you know I was swimming?"

"Bridget."

"Ah, right. To answer your question, no, with an ocean right outside, there's no indoor pool." He pinched a slice of her bacon, then held it up for her to take a bite. Mouth full, she forgot her next question.

"I've thought a lot," he admitted, "about what you said last night, and you're right. So, the PR people have scheduled a press conference for late this afternoon in front of the Boston offices. I'll reassure the staff, thank the first responders, inspectors, and engineers. Like you said."

She felt heat crawl up her neck and knew her face was pink. He'd listened to her? And even more, taken her advice? What about his overprotective need to keep her safe?

Like a mind-reader, he said, "I'm still concerned about your safety but if you don't mind Ryan tagging along?"

"No, what a great idea. I like Ryan; he seems extremely competent."

"He is. Well, he can drive us to town for a little shopping, then drop me off and take you to Vic's during the press conference. Finally, come back to pick me up. Does that suit you?"

"That suits me perfectly," she said with a laugh. Leaping to her feet, she rounded the table and pressed a kiss on his lips. Her instant bolt of desire worked as a warning. She jerked back, murmuring, "Sorry."

On his feet, Murdoch grabbed her shoulders and held her in front of him.

"Annalisa, don't ever apologize for kissing me. I should be the one begging your pardon for letting surprise ruin my response."

"That wasn't ruined," she whispered.

"I'll be better prepared next time. If you're rationing kisses, I'll make damn sure each one counts."

A short time later, she sat beside Murdoch in the back of a new-smelling Cadillac Escalade. "Driving a black SUV?" she observed. "Like an FBI agent on TV."

"I took out the two center seats," Ryan said from the behind the wheel. "So you'd have more leg room," his voice dropped, "plus it makes for better security."

She swung her head to check Murdoch's face. He scowled at Ryan via the rearview mirror.

"Where shall we stop first?" Murdoch asked her, in an obvious change of topic. "Beacon Hill?" His tactic worked. Wasn't Beacon Hill the Rodeo Drive of Boston?

She put her lips next to his ear. "Too expensive."

"I've got plastic."

"Don't you dare *Pretty Woman* me."

"The scene with the store manager sucking up was hilarious." Murdoch darted a quick look at her face and said, "No, no way. I'd never try that. Wouldn't dream of it. We'll keep a strict account of all the receipts and split the total when you get your Muirdris reimbursement payment."

The first boutique had a large SALE sign in the front window. "How about this one?" She pointed.

Inside the store, Murdoch looked around. "If I

join you in the little room, you won't have to parade around in front of the whole store."

"Very thoughtful, but no thanks. I won't be long." She chose three pairs of designer jeans all in different cuts, and a stylish wrap dress that caught her eye. She was shocked when everything fit perfectly. The dress looked great but at 50 percent off, it was still more money than she'd ever paid for a single item of clothing. She turned to study her butt again in the mirrors. It fit like it was custom made for her. Maybe she could afford to start buying better clothes with her raise.

She smoothed the skirt down over her wide hips. What would Murdoch say about the dress? Stepping out of the *little room*, she noticed him standing beside a sales clerk and signaled to him. No need to ask if he liked the dress. His eyes lit up like Fourth of July fireworks.

He discreetly palmed an AX card to her and whispered, "Use this one, please. It keeps a strict account of the charges." At the register, she concentrated on signing for the purchases and tried not to hyperventilate at the total.

The next stop was at a larger store where the stock included sweaters, tops, accessories, and hats. She carefully chose one long sleeved top and a sweater she could wear now and would transition back to Southern California weather when she went home.

Murdoch moved behind her and rested his chin on her shoulder to whisper, "You need a real coat to protect you when it freezes and snows. Please let me buy one for you." When his warm breath caressed her ear and cheek, Annalisa shivered. She couldn't turn her head; his mouth was right there.

"I'll agree to try on a couple," she whispered, "if you promise not to go crazy."

He led her to the rack of heavy and lined coats. "What's your favorite color?"

"In most cases it's blue, but not in outerwear. I like that grey puffy one and the camel colored."

"Maybe you should consider wearing bright colors. I think you'll like it. Let's try one combination, see if you approve." He held up a coat, she slid her arms in and he stopped her from turning to face the mirror. "Not yet. Wait to see it all together."

For a moment he kept his arms around her waist, his mouth back to her earlobe again. He nuzzled beneath her ear and she jerked back. "Not in public," she hissed. "What if someone recognizes you? Every person in this store has a camera in their phone."

He held his hands up. "I'll be good. Now keep an open mind about vibrant colors."

He wrapped a soft knit scarf around her neck, slid matching mittens on her hands and placed a knit cap over her hair. "Now look."

She gasped at the image in the mirror. The blue coat, in a mock military style that complimented her full figure, featured red and purple trim. The red, white and purple yarn of the scarf, hat and mittens created a put-together look she seldom managed to attain, but decided she loved.

"Sold." She circled her arms around his waist intending to give him a thank you hug. He dropped his mouth on hers, kissed her hard.

Photo flashes erupted around them. People taking pictures of them kissing.

Chapter Eleven

Murdoch circled his arm around his mate's shoulders, tucked her closer, and made a bee-line for the exit. He was clear-headed enough to pry the AX card from Annalisa's frozen grip and toss it to the sales clerk.

"I'll send someone for the receipt and the other stuff she wanted." Once he and Annalisa were out of sight in the SUV, he'd send Ryan back in.

As he hustled Annalisa out of the store, Ryan hurried forward. The SUV was right in front, double-parked and the security chief had the door to the Escalade standing open. Something in Ryan's face triggered a decision in Murdoch.

He'd spent all of his adult life in Murphy's shadow. Always the younger twin, never the chieftain. And the few times he'd tried to match his brother's business talents, his projects had failed. Or turned out less profitable than projected. Finally, he avoided assignments for fear the next task he'd seriously screw up. Lose some of the clan's hoard.

As of today, his half-hearted efforts or avoidance were no longer acceptable. Failure was not an option, as the saying went. He'd found his mate and she believed in him. Well, she liked him and wanted to have confidence in him. And she would believe in him if he started getting things right, taking full responsibility for his actions. That started right here, right now.

He handed Annalisa off to Ryan. "Lock the car and make sure she's warm. I'll be right out with our purchases."

He turned on his heel and returned to the store. At the register, he raised a hand. "Hello, everyone, may I have your attention?"

The giggles and chatter stopped.

"If any of you intend to tag those pictures you just took, my name is Murdoch, m-u-r-d-o-c-h, Rudraige, part owner of Muirdris Shipping. I'm not Murphy, he's my twin brother."

"Holy shit, they *are* identical twins."

"Two of them look like that?"

"I'd say this one's taken."

"Hey Murdoch," one woman shouted, "Who's the woman?"

"Sorry, above all, I'm a gentleman. Thank you." He signed the charge slip, hung the bags over his arm, and waved as he went out the door.

The Escalade was gone. *Son of a bitch.* Instant karma? Be a better man and you'll walk home? A horn beeped, and the SUV screeched to a stop in front of him. Gesturing Ryan to stay where he was, Murdoch hopped into the back seat and put his arm around Annalisa. She sipped water from a reusable Muirdris bottle.

"Are you okay?" he asked.

"I could use another minute or two."

He gave her a slight squeeze, sat back, and tried to think like a human woman. What could he do to make things easier for her? She'd warned him about all the cameras and she'd been correct. It was his fault for not listening, his fault for kissing her in public. But was she saying *I told you so*? No, his beautiful mate was simply unhappy.

Show her the Hoard, the dragon insisted. Right. His beast's simple remedy for all of life's ills. Bask in their beautiful treasure and you'll feel much better.

Earlier today, while Annalisa slept, he'd performed a high-dive off the living room terrace. Just before he plunged into the ocean, he'd shifted to his sea dragon. His shifts, especially the mid-air ones, were exhilarating, liberating and only slightly uncomfortable as his body began to stretch the moment before he completely transformed.

He raced submerged down the shoreline, knowing his dragon was invisible to human eyes, while he'd scared the shit out of several schools of fish and a seal. Backtracking, he made his way to his cliffs and inside to the hidden cave. Once the sea dragon had crawled up onto the flat rocks, he'd shifted back to his human form, clothes intact. Another extremely handy mythical gene they'd all inherited from the Dragon line.

He'd gone to his cave to restore the Celtic coin to its place of honor on the heap of precious stones and coins. That done, he'd moved to the piles of jewelry to choose a gift for Annalisa. A gift worthy of his mate.

And that was another problem. He and the dragon couldn't wait to see her dripping in his collections of emeralds, covered in ropes of pearls, adorned in diamonds. But, fearful she'd refuse expensive, he'd searched for something simple. Anything she'd accept and wear. All the while, his dragon roared his disapproval.

The best. Our mate must have the best!

Reasoning seldom worked. "Be patient, big guy. Humans take time. I'll explain everything to her—soon."

Now, sitting beside her in the car, Murdoch reached into his pocket and touched the modest silver pendant he'd finally chosen and brought with him.

"How long do you think it'll take before one of those pictures, tagged with both our names, shows up on line?" Annalisa asked him while she continued to stare out the tinted window.

He looked up and his gaze met Ryan's in the rearview. "I don't know."

Lowering his voice to a whisper, he spoke close to her ear. "I've been thinking about this since last night. Tell me if you agree."

She tipped her head closer to his lips. At least she was willing to listen.

"The more I learn about you, discover, the more I like and the more I want to know."

"I feel the same way," she admitted. His heart leapt. "Discovering your personality, your favorite things, how you react in different situations, it's wonderful."

"My brother should be back by next week. That'll open up more options for us. If you miss home, Murphy could take over the spy hunt and you and I could go to Los Angeles together."

"Is that what you want?"

"No, actually. I want the both of us to see this through, together. Finish the project and identify the bad guy. But if you–"

"Me too, I want to stay."

"Great. I think we should contact HR. Inform them we're dating, like it says in the manual. Not in a relationship but dating. You'll still decide what and how much physical contact we have. That way, as we're getting closer, you never have to worry about losing your job or any of the Muirdris rules like that."

"Seems like a big step."

"Happens every day. This is a huge company. All HR wants to avoid is a relationship between two people where one reports to the other. Or to be blindsided by a harassment lawsuit."

"I didn't exactly think of it that way."

"Once HR is made aware, then the direction this friendship or relationship takes will be based solely on our decisions. For example, whenever you want to kiss me, you can go right ahead." Annalisa's cheeks glowed with a rosy blush.

"Personally," he continued, "I want us to move forward in this friendship. Hoping it'll quickly progress into a relationship. What do you think?"

"I think that's a very logical plan."

He stuck out his bottom lip in an exaggerated pout. "Logical?"

"Actually, progress is a wonderful idea."

"Better," he growled and lifted his head. "Ryan,

contact Trace, supervisor of human resources. Tell him we'll pick him up across the street from the Muirdris main entrance, ten minutes after the press conference ends."

"Right, Murdoch."

He eased Annalisa closer, kissed her on the neck. "Before you and Ryan drop me off at the press conference and you go to Vic's house, we've got to make one more special purchase."

"Oh? Right, we forgot PJ's."

He laughed. "No, but that's not a bad idea." A mental image of a half-naked Annalisa flashed through his brain. She squirmed on his bed, moaning like she did when he kissed her, as he peeled off her pajama bottoms using only his teeth.

"What are we buying?"

"We're officiating at the christening of Muirdris's newest ship. Followed by an extremely formal, entirely stuffy ball. Did you bring a gown?"

"Seriously?"

"Excuse me, Murdoch?" Ryan said from the front, "We don't have time for another stop. Need to get you to the press conference."

"Step on it, Ryan." He tugged Annalisa into his arms and kissed her. She parted her lips, inviting him in. His tongue delved into that sweet mouth and she quietly groaned her approval. As the kiss deepened, Annalisa's hands slid under his shirt where she stroked the bare skin of his back. *Progress*.

He angled himself to shield her from the rearview mirror. The hand that was out of Ryan's view wandered beneath the side hem of her sweater and under the tank top as he caressed the soft velvety flesh of her midriff. Moving higher beneath the layers, he cupped one generous mound. Damn, his mate's plump breast over flowed in his hand. Tracing his thumb over the taut nipple, Murdoch was rewarded with another groan. He broke the kiss to dart a look at Ryan's profile. His security chief kept his eyes straight ahead.

"Two blocks," Ryan announced in a subdued tone.

Oh shit. He needed a cold shower.

"Tuck your shirt in," Annalisa said, adjusting her sweater.

"Are you okay?" he asked her.

"Don't worry about me, where's your tie?"

"Sir, your suit jacket and tie are in the garment bag right behind the seat."

He and Annalisa both turned and lunged for the bag, barely avoiding a collision.

"Sit back, Sweetling," he said kindly, "I've got this." He managed to finish dressing and secure his tie as Ryan slowed for traffic congesting the street to the building.

"Boss, check out that crowd," Ryan spoke quickly. "If the lady can stay out of sight, we should make a splash for your arrival."

"What do you have in mind?" he asked while beside him Annalisa grinned and nodded.

"After I pull to the curb, wait for one of Ji's men to open the door back there. Annalisa, all you have to do is keep your head down and turned away from Murdoch's open door. Next I'll take you to Vic's. After the press conference is over, we'll be back to pick Murdoch up the same way."

Murdoch raised an eyebrow at Annalisa, she gave him two thumbs up.

Ryan stopped the Escalade at the curb. Ji himself approached the car and with a nod from Ryan, swung open Murdoch's door, and stood at attention.

Murdoch counted to ten. Stepped onto the sidewalk and into a wall of sound: applause, shouted questions, cheers. And an explosion of lights: floods, TV cameras, photo flashes.

Chapter Twelve

Annalisa curled up on the sofa across from Vic. The VP's townhouse was exactly what she'd expected a top executive at Muirdris to own. And it was walking distance to work. Was her secure space in this building?

The only puzzling pieces of décor, like *which one doesn't belong*? All the paintings, prints, etchings, even woodcuts featured forests and woodland scenes chock full of small wild creatures. Maybe Vic was related to Snow White.

They'd watched the press conference and subsequent questions and answers session, televised live on a local TV channel. Murdoch had been perfect. He looked good enough to eat. Sounded sexy as hell. Maybe she was a trifle biased. He'd certainly come across as strong yet humble and caring and grateful.

Vic's phone beeped. "A text from Murdoch. *Crowd is wicked crazy. I'll pick up HR Lance, bring him there. After Lance, we finish shopping. Or eat, then shop.*

Up to you. XXOO."

Vic's eyebrow arched.

Certain her warm face was pink with blushing, Annalisa hurried to say, "I'm sorry we're intruding. We're shopping for my replacement phone."

"You must be going nuts without it."

"I am."

Vic rose and said, "Do you think Ryan will come inside this time?"

"I have no idea." It was her turn trying to read Vic's expression. The woman was a sphinx.

Vic gestured to the hallway. "Would excuse me? If I'm entertaining Murdoch and the head of HR, I need to do a quick tidy-up."

Starting to push up from the couch, Annalisa asked, "Can I help?"

"No, relax, put your feet up," Vic said. "I'll be back in a couple minutes."

Alone in the quiet living room, Annalisa sipped lukewarm coffee and considered Murdoch. What was her next step? She'd forgiven him for lying about his identity. And she admired the heck out of his desire to stick with it until they found the conspirator selling protocols. Still, on the personal front, despite what he *said*, he was definitely rushing her. Maybe because once she returned home, she'd be thousands of miles away? Still, what was this thing between them? Emotions changing and moving at light speed. Was that a good thing or bad? *Damn it.* She had a reputation for logical thought. Right now, her brain was acting like a tilt-a-whirl. How could she be this crazy about someone she didn't know all that well?

Before she'd arrived at any earth-shattering decisions, the doorbell rang. *Crap.* Now she got to bare her personal life to Muirdris's head of the HR department.

Interrogation over, back in the Escalade, Annalisa chose to return to the village near Murdoch's mansion for dinner and then gown shopping. Murdoch made several calls he assured her would smooth their way. Seemed the man was determined to spoil her.

By the time the remains of their salads were whisked away, and the main dinner course arrived, she'd managed to seriously relax. "You were amazing at the press conference."

Murdoch shook his head. "It was a mistake to let that reporter bait me into answering a question about fuel consumption on our older vessels."

"What are you supposed to do? Ignore him?"

"Ignore or say no comment. Or re-direct the question. Remind everyone how great the mileage is on our new ships. And our commitment to the goals of the

Paris Accord."

"I thought your answer was inspired." She waited to hear him say her judgement didn't count. Instead, he kissed her hand and said, "Yours is the opinion I care most about. So, I'm happy."

After dessert, Murdoch texted Ryan to pick them up.

Stepping outside was like walking to a frozen meat locker. "Smells like snow," Murdoch observed, bundling them into the car. "Ryan?"

"I know, more heat."

Then, instead of driving Ryan leaned over the backrest and announced, "Ran into Chief O'Malley at the Thai place. He's full of good news. The State police arrested a man they believe stole the truck and rear-ended Annalisa's rental car."

"Good news," Murdoch said. "We should celebrate. Who is he?"

"Wait, there's more," Ryan continued, "No positive ID yet, however, the guy's talking pretty weird. Based on a couple things he let slip, he could've also planted the car bomb in the Muirdris parking garage."

"Two for one? That is great news."

Ryan held up a finger. "Until they know for sure this is the guy, O'Malley strongly recommends we continue all our precautions for Annalisa."

Murdoch, his arm around her shoulders, asked, "It that okay with you?"

"Yes," she smiled. "I appreciate the security."

Murdoch glanced up to Ryan. "Next stop, we're looking for a ship christening gown for Annalisa. Both of the high-end shops in the village are expecting us. And Ryan, I think you should come in with us. The temperature is still plummeting."

"I will. Thanks."

Inside the first boutique, Annalisa discovered that in Murdoch's world *smoothing the way* meant an owner unlocking her store after closing it for the evening, pulling five gowns that met his criteria, and readying the dresses for Annalisa to try on.

She sat with Murdoch on an ornate love seat. The owner said, "Let me show you what I've selected, and you decide which ones you'd like to try on." She held up number one, a dazzling white gown with a fitted beaded bodice and flared skirt.

"Sorry, no," Annalisa said. "It looks too much like a wedding dress."

"You'd look spectacular in white," the owner said, "Your skin is such a golden tan."

"Could I see the green one? It reminds me of the ocean."

The shop owner held up a gown in a mermaid cut.

Annalisa's heart sank. The fitted fabric from waist to knees was never going to fit over her hips.

"It's beautiful. And slinky. Do you have it in one size larger?"

"No, I'm sorry. Would you like to try it on?"

"Before we go there," Annalisa said, "tell me the price of the dress."

"It's an original. One of a kind at $14,990."

She didn't gasp, didn't even flinch. Lots of fabulously wealthy people lived in southern California, working in the entertainment industry, big business. Extremely rich people who could afford haute couture pricing. She swallowed. People like Murdoch.

"Annalisa?" Murdoch took her hand. "Don't worry about—"

She stood, tugging him up with her. "Ma'am, please excuse us. We'll only be a moment." Turning back to Murdoch she whispered, "Could I have a word with you? In private?"

Dropping his hand, she marched to a far corner of the store. "Stop doing this," she demanded, her voice low and flat. "It feels like you're trying to buy me. You must know I can't afford my half of that dress. It—"

"You're angry at me because I want you to have nice things? Like a beautiful dress to wear on a special occasion? That's not trying to buy you. That's trying to make you happy."

"Listen carefully. Spending money isn't the best route to happiness. I'd be just as happy with a $1000 dress. I understand it's a special occasion. I know I need to look great standing next to my billionaire boss. But if I have to wear a $15,000 dress? It's not going to work. Actually, I don't ever need or want anything that expensive."

"I don't understand. Why wouldn't you want—"

"I know you don't get it; don't get me. That's the really sad part." She bowed her head for a moment. He didn't say a word. "Why don't I explain my price range to the owner? Let her find different dresses for me to try on?"

Murdoch walked away from her, across the thick carpet without a backward glance. Annalisa returned to speak to the boutique owner and smash the woman's hopes for a huge sale.

Chapter Thirteen

Murdoch waited by the front display window while Annalisa told the shop owner what she wanted. The woman glanced his way, He gave her a quick nod and she disappeared into the stock room presumably in search of economical gowns. A few feet away, Ryan's head peeked around the edge of a decorative divider.

"Can we talk?" the security chief asked in a low whisper.

"Sure. What's on your mind?"

"It's none of my business, but— "

"Crappy start, Ryan, just spit it out. We've been friends for a long time. I'm not going to sack you now."

"Just making sure. Honestly, I've never seen you like this. Bouncing back and forth, from one extreme to the other. You finally volunteered for a press conference and stepped off the podium looking like a fucking rock star. At the same time, you're making truly horrible personal decisions about Annalisa.

What the hell's going on with you?"

"It's all her. I'm crazy about her and the woman has me tied up in knots. She's in danger because of a Muirdris issue she uncovered in California. I'll tell you all the details tomorrow morning. The rest, like the press briefing…" Murdoch trailed off.

"Let me guess. You're finally becoming the man we all knew you could be, just by living up to her expectations?"

"You make it sound damn simple."

"Nah, love is never uncomplicated."

"How do I get the woman a ball gown for tomorrow night? Why would she turn down my offer to buy one for her?"

"Because this isn't the 19th century? Or the 20th."

Murdoch furrowed his forehead. "I support equality, her right to vote, that—"

"Back up," Ryan had both his hands up. "It's not about politics with you two. Problem is, you've been pushing too hard and making her less and less happy that you're extremely rich."

"What can I do about—?"

"In my opinion, Annalisa cares about you and she sees you as an okay guy. But, thanks in big part to all that money, you have a reputation for messing up. You're rich, why bother putting in the work? Besides,

Murphy can do it better, faster, cheaper. With one hand tied behind his back."

"Can't he?"

"So can you, my friend. And, big point, the money is not the real cause of your problems, but she thinks it is. Solution, you need to go ahead and become that better man, despite the money."

"And I'm going about that all wrong?"

"Yep. By throwing money at her, you're hoping to win her faster. Instead, you're reinforcing every one of her fears. Demonstrating that because you're so rich, you haven't developed any real feelings."

Murdoch pursed his lips. "Annalisa would rather I put in the time and effort instead of using my money."

"Bingo." Ryan slapped him on the shoulder. "I realize it might go against your nature—"

"What?" *Did Ryan know what he secretly was? Or even suspect?*

"Just saying," Ryan backpedaled. "Changing your attitude might not be so easy."

"And yet, the faster I chain down my urges to spend buckets of money on Annalisa, the faster she'll accept the real me."

"Considering your need for speed, you might consider jumpstarting that campaign."

"Suggestions?"

"It needs to be something big. A clear demonstration of how you feel—"

"Without directly spending any money on her," Murdoch finished for Ryan, smacking his new confidant on the back. "I know exactly what to do. And I can start right now." Grinning ear to ear, he asked Ryan, "Would you warm up the car and meet us outside?"

"Want me to call the other store? Cancel your appointment?"

"Yes, thanks."

Murdoch strolled back to the small sofa, leaned over to Annalisa. "I think it's time to regroup. Start over on the plans for the Christening ball, what do you say?"

"How can you do that? It's tomorrow night and I still need a dress."

"Will you meet me in the big dressing room? After I apologize to you, we'll discuss the ball."

"No apology's neces—"

"In the room that says Bridal. I'll be with you in a minute."

He found the owner in the stock room, begged her forgiveness. "We'll be back another time, give you more notice."

"Anytime, Mr. Rudraige. Tap on my office door when you're ready to leave."

He stopped in the fitting room doorway. Annalisa sat ramrod straight on a little flowered chair. "I sincerely apologize for trying to saddle you with a dress that costs more than you're comfortable paying. Please believe me, I'm not trying to buy you."

Stepping into the room, he softly closed the door. "For many generations my family, the men, have shown their love by giving gifts. It's our custom, a tradition, to literally shower the woman he loves with the most expensive gifts a man can afford. I'm not sharing this background with you to give myself an excuse, but because it may be a difficult pattern to break. I might need reminding if I start to screw up again."

"Murdoch? You just said, the woman he loves. That tradition can't possibly apply to—"

"Please, let me take one step at a time. Now do you understand where my excessive behavior is coming from? Can you believe that from now on, I'll do my very best to change? And accept my apology for making you uncomfortable?"

"Well, yes. I can understand diverse customs. Acknowledge that people view money and gift-giving very differently. I admire your determination to change and accept your apology."

"Good." *Whew*. He had made it past a tough part. Now to explain fated mates. Tomorrow, he'd introduce her to his sea dragon. Was that rushing her?

He sank down onto a stool, closer to Annalisa and at eye level. "The Celtic clan Murphy and I come from believes in love at first sight. And we're told that each one of us has a soulmate."

"Love at first sight? I don't know. Those instances are more likely to be cases of instant chemistry. I must admit, the idea of having a soulmate somewhere out there is intriguing."

He took one of her hands. Turning it over, he lifted it to his lips, and kissed the center of her palm.

"I knew I loved you, Annalisa, the minute I lifted you out of the crushed car. I know you're my soulmate."

She opened her mouth. He gently squeezed her hand to stop her. "Let me say, most hu…um, people would say it's too soon to decide I'm in love. Then again, the soulmate part helps. I know you're the one."

"Oh lord. That explains so much. No wonder you keep trying to spend buckets of money on me."

"Exactly." He grinned. She gave him a hesitant smile back. Then her lips turned down, and she whispered, "Tell the truth. Are you disappointed I can't say it back to you?"

"Only a little. I can also appreciate other traditions and different customs. Could I have my *you're forgiven* hug?" He waggled his eyebrows at her, longing to see the sweet smile light up her face again.

She waggled right back. "Just a hug?"

"I'll take anything you want to give. Honestly, I'm happy with forgiveness, understanding, and a hug."

Standing up to embrace him, her smile was back. And just as quickly vanished. Again. *Love with a fated mate was a damn roller coaster*.

"Murdoch, what about a dress for the ball?"

That he could handle. "Sweetling, from here on, I intend to consult you on every important decision. Starting right after I implement this one." He moved aside, tapped a number in his phone. "This is for you," he mouthed to Annalisa. "Eliminating the need for an expensive dress."

He spoke into the phone, "Liz? It's Murdoch. Sorry to call so last minute. It's about the Ball. I need you to send a group text and follow it up with an email to all the ticket holders. We're offering a new, alternative dress code as an option for tomorrow night. Either the traditional black tie, or dress jeans and a sweatshirt. Yes…yes, let me finish. Ji will award a $1000 prize for the most obscure college sweatshirt, and another grand for the losing-est sports team logo on a sweatshirt. Make the announcement and thanks, Liz. See you tomorrow night. I'll bring the prize money in cash."

After he'd texted the news to Ji, before he could pocket his phone, a laughing Annalisa walked straight into his arms. *Damn, his plan was working.*

"Murdoch," she whispered. "Hug me quick." She curled her arms around his neck and tangled her fingers in his hair. He hauled her tighter against him, savoring the voluptuous curves as they pressed to his body.

Lowering his chin for a kiss, he discovered Annalisa was shaking with laughter. He tipped his head back. "What?"

"You are the most spoiled man on the face of the Earth."

Chapter Fourteen

The interior of the Escalade was toasty warm when Annalisa slipped into the back with Murdoch right behind her. Through the tinted side-window, she gave the long-suffering boutique owner, busy locking up the store, a goodbye wave.

As the car pulled away from the curb, Murdoch slid an arm around her shoulders but instead of resuming their kiss, he frowned. "Want to explain now what was so funny?"

"Can Ryan hear us?" she mouthed.

"Hey Ryan," he raised his voice. "How about turning on some background music?"

"Will do." In the front, Ryan chose a jazz station, increased the volume and tipped the rearview mirror aside.

Seemingly satisfied they'd achieved as much privacy as possible, Murdoch turned back to her, keeping his voice to a whisper. "Look, I'll admit I might be a little spoiled, but the worst in the world?"

"You listened to my objections about spending money on me. Said you understood. And on the surface, your idea to expand the ball's dress code so I'd be comfortable? A really sweet gesture. But then, without a blink, you decided to spend two thousand dollars to make it happen? For a few hours in jeans?"

"It's a fun contest for the people attending the…"

"Two thousand?"

"Think of the thousands I'll save by not buying that dress."

"You know that's beside the point." She watched as changing expressions zipped across his chiseled face. He was trying to see her logic, her side. When his eyes widened, her heart swelled. Murdoch might not agree, but at least he got it.

With a short nod, he said, "So, I spent money to get what I wanted. Bought my way…"

She stopped his words with her mouth. Heart thudding, she was thrilled with his ability to adapt.

The instant her lips pressed to his, Murdoch seemed to get down to business. One of his large hands grasped the back of her neck, adjusted the angle of her head, and he deepened the kiss. His tongue slid between her lips and plunged into her mouth. Taking turns, their tongues darted in and around the wet shadowy depths, dueling, teasing and arousing. She was awash with waves of pleasure.

His other muscular arm encircled her waist, urging her closer. She couldn't remember ever being this turned on and was ready to crawl all over his body, but the setting wasn't *that* private. Instead, she arched her back, rubbed her breasts against his chest, heightening her desire even more. Judging by his loud groan, Murdoch felt the same.

Shit, Ryan would hear them. A bubble of embarrassed laughter rose in her throat.

Murdoch slowly withdrew his lips from hers, then sprinkled butterfly kisses across her cheek until he reached the soft skin under her earlobe. The brush of his short beard against her skin sent goose bumps springing up all over her body. She imagined his facial hair rubbing other parts of her body and her nipples ached.

When his mouth didn't move any lower than her neck, her brain started to clear. *No, don't stop.* "Murdoch?" she whispered in his ear. "What is it?" He couldn't be worried about Ryan overhearing them. Something else? A sinking feel of dread lodged in the pit of her stomach. Now that she was all in, he'd changed his mind?

Bringing his head up, he cupped his hands on either side of her face, dropped a light kiss on her mouth. When he tipped his head back, she focused on his eyes, and tried to read his mind.

"Everything is exactly right," he whispered, his breath tickling her mouth. "It's just that I don't want any more misunderstandings. I want us to make love, tonight, all night. Tell me, is that what you want?"

Relief flooded through her, re-fueling her desire. "Yes Murdoch, I want you, too. Just not in the car, with Ryan driving. We need privacy, a bed. As soon as we get home, let's go to your bedroom and have sex. Do you have condoms?"

He choked on a laugh. "Yes, lots of condoms, a California king-sized bed, and an overwhelming desire to make love with you again and again, for the rest of the night."

"Sounds perfect. Exactly how far are we from the house?"

He glanced out the side window. "Four minutes."

As the SUV swept through the newly repaired front gate, he asked in a husky voice, "Mind if I carry you upstairs? I can run faster."

He took the stairs two at a time and they made it as far as the doorway of his bedroom. When Murdoch paused to kick the door closed, she raked her teeth across his earlobe. He let out a loud groan and started peeling off her clothing. Without the support of his arms, she slid down his body, landing on her feet. He gripped her shoulders, pressed her back against the closed door and ravished her mouth.

She scrambled to pull off his shirt, unhook and unzip his pants. At the sound of the zipper, he muttered what sounded like, "Wait."

Damn it, now what? "Something wrong?"

"Nothing's wrong with you, Sweetling, you're amazing. Which is why I need our first time together to be—"

"Aww Murdoch, you're hesitant to nail me up against the wall? Such a romantic."

*   *   *

Murdoch

"Quit giving me a hard time," Murdoch warned. Stepping out of the pants pooled around his ankles, he tossed Annalisa's almost naked body over one shoulder, caveman style, and had them beside the bed in three long strides. He knelt on the edge of the mattress, worked his way to the middle, and laid Annalisa, his treasure, our mate, down in the center of the bed.

Braced above her, he slowly raked his eyes down

the length of her body, her luscious curves clad in only in her new red bra and matching panties. She squirmed.

"You are beyond beautiful," he told her.

His dragon roared, fighting to be released.

No. Murdoch growled back at his beast. *This is my part. I'll introduce you tomorrow and you can show off for our mate.*

Murdoch reached beneath Annalisa, unhooked the bra and tossed it to the floor. Then, starting with the spot under her ear, kissed and nuzzled his way down her neck and sternum until he reached those abundant breasts. Gently cupping one he gave it a little squeeze and watched the nipple grow taut. Annalisa moaned encouragement while she dug her fingernails into his shoulders.

He licked a wet swath over the tight nipple and she gasped. He gently teased the surrounding puckered flesh with his teeth, then sucked hard, drawing the peak and a portion of her breast deep into his mouth. She arched to him, offering and murmuring, "Yes, Murdoch. More."

Determined to drive her wild, he teased and suckled first one breast, then the other until both nipples were wet, stiff peaks that strained toward him. She was so sensitive, so responsive. Could he bring her to the first climax this way? By only worshiping and stimulating her breasts? He swept his tongue over the silky skin of each mound and reveled in the sounds of pleasure she made.

Finally, he couldn't ignore the scent of her arousal any longer. It was too sweet and beckoned him lower, to her core. Running his tongue along the top edge of her damp panties, he heard Annalisa's gasping breath catch.

Murdoch hooked his fingers over the elastic, slid her underwear off, and sent it arching to the floor next to the matching bra. With her knees spread wide open, her enticing center completely exposed, he couldn't stop staring. "You're magnificent. Your pussy looks delicious." Moving to kneel between her legs, he placed her ankles up over his shoulders, and supported her butt with one hand.

Inhaling her unique, tantalizing aroma as he kissed his way down her inner thighs, he murmured, "Can't wait to taste you." With his free hand he spread her wet folds apart, then explored the edges with his tongue. "Delectable."

When her thighs trembled, and she squirmed with anticipation, Murdoch lapped at the opening of her pussy and then to her waiting clit.

She screamed, "Right there," and he obeyed,

working her clit by flicking it with the tip of his tongue. Once he'd established a rhythmic pattern. he trust one finger deep into her slick heat.

"Yes," she begged, rocking her hips, "I need you inside me."

He slowly withdrew the finger then thrust it fully into her again. As her breathing became panting, he added a second finger, and increased the speed.

"Don't stop," she begged. "I'm coming."

Her orgasm was just as breathtaking for him Her inner muscles throbbed and squeezed on his fingers. He could easily imagine those sensations on his cock. Continuing to flick with his tongue, fingers thrusting, he drew out her climax.

Finally, she gasped, "No more."

Gently placing her legs on the bedspread, he crawled up beside her and enveloped her in his arms. He kissed her lightly as tiny aftershocks made her tremble.

What had he ever done to deserve such a woman? Such a life mate? She exhaled a deep sigh. The woman positively glowed with contentment. Annalisa shifted her legs and pressed into his hard cock.

"Whoa. All that just for me?" She teased and reached for him, "My turn."

He circled one hand around her wrist, stopped

her hand. "Let's save that for later. Right now, I want to watch you come apart with me buried deep inside you."

"If you insist."

Chapter Fifteen

Her heart still racing from the first epic orgasm, Annalisa watched Murdoch through half-closed lids as he retrieved a condom from the bedside table and returned to smile down at her.

He placed the unopened packet on top of her pubic bone and stretched out beside her. Then he rolled himself halfway on top of her. Teasing her mouth with quick little pretend nips and long sensuous licks, while stroking her hair with his free hand, Murdoch managed to fire her body heat and lust level right back up to pre-orgasmic. Assaulting her mouth with deep, wet mouth invasions, he gave new meaning to French kissing.

Stroking her hair with his hands and tracing her skin with fingertips added another layer to their lovemaking. Caring and affection became a part of the white-hot passion that raced through her body.

Murdoch trailed his mouth lower and sucked her

nipple deep into his mouth. She groaned as the sensation resonated in her core.

When his stroking hand delved into her wet folds and teased her clit exactly the way she liked it, Annalisa felt her body stiffen. Just before she melted into the climax, she glanced down to see her breast in Murdoch's mouth and his shining eyes watching her. Then all she saw was stars.

Again, he prolonged her orgasm. When she started breathing again, he sucked harder on her nipple while he stroked her hip and up and down her thigh.

She lifted her hips. "Now, I need you inside me." Her movements slid the condom packet across her pelvis. "You know, that's not how those work."

He released her nipple with a popping sound and grinned. "Why don't you show me?"

"No problem." She sat up and ripped open the packet. She'd never rolled one of these on a man, but she'd seen it done before. *Oh lordy.* Murdoch was huge. And bonus, as she worked the ribbed latex over his bobbing cock, the lovely thing got bigger.

Protection in place, he took charge again. He plundered her mouth, pressing his body to hers until she was flat on her back. Then he drew up, kneeling between her thighs, and took in the view. "You are amazing."

He gripped her thighs, guiding her legs to encircle his hips. Teasing the head of his cock over her clit, he finally positioned himself at her entrance.

"Yes?" he gasped.

She tipped her hips, inviting him in. "Stop teasing. Fill me. Now."

Without a word, he slid his cock deep inside her. They moaned in unison. He filled her and more.

"Fuck yeah." He began to move, drawing back until only the head of his cock remained inside, then he thrust into her again, balls deep.

"Oh god, yes." She was on fire. "Again." At this moment, she needed what he was giving her more than her next breath.

*   *   *

Murdoch

Murdoch was going crazy with all the sensations, both outside and inside of his body. As he slammed into Annalisa, her breasts moved in time to his thrusts and inside him the dragon went wild. *Our mate. Claim her.*

He gulped for air, barely able to catch his breath. His heart beat against his chest like a storm pounding the cliffs below his house. Every little sound from his expressive mate drove him closer to his climax. *Wait, together.*

She planted her feet on the mattress, tipped her hips to meet his thrusts. Her nails raked his shoulders and down over his chest tattoo. "Close," she moaned.

He slid his open palm across her rock-hard nipple. And almost set himself off.

"Yes," Annalisa brushed his hand aside and tugged on her own nipple. He had to look away or come right then. She was so fucking hot.

He pulled back until only the tip of his cock remained in her, changed the angle of penetration and thrust deep.

"Yes," she screamed. "Yes, Murdoch. Right there." And she climaxed. Her inner muscles gripped his cock, pulsing with her satisfaction. She threw back her head, letting out a long low moan. The sight was too much for him. He gave one final thrust and emptied himself deep inside his mate.

I love you, I love you, repeated over and over through his head.

He collapsed on the bed beside Annalisa, one of his arms and a leg draped over her. When he could breathe again, he lifted his head to check on Annalisa.

"Still here," she teased. "When you go to the bathroom to clean up, bring me a glass of water?"

After he'd disposed of the condom, he brought her water and several extra pillows. Propping the pillows against the headboard, he sat and patted the spot next to him. He held her water steady while she scooted up to join him. After he looped his arm around her shoulders, she snuggled against his chest.

Handing over the water, he asked, "This is cuddling?"

"Yes, but people can cuddle most anywhere. This is more accurately referred to as pillow talk."

"Talk that happens while you're in bed?"

"Well, the subtext is talk during the afterglow of good sex, when couples share deep secrets."

"And we just had good sex—right?"

"Phenomenal sex. I'll tell you anything. What secrets do you want me to spill?"

"Actually, I have a secret to show you tomorrow."

"That's exciting, but it doesn't count as pillow talk. Could I ask you a personal question?"

"Anything."

"Ji and Lance and even Vic seem surprised by the success of your press conference. Would you tell me why? Or was it just my imagination?"

"I don't mind explaining. Before I met you, my

soulmate, in any comparisons between me and Murphy, I usually came out the loser. After a while, I quit competing." Murdoch swallowed hard. Couldn't believe what he'd just said. That he'd exposed such a deep, raw place. On one hand, he was proud he'd told his mate a secret truth, on the other hand, he wanted her to think only the best of him.

He hesitated long enough to check her expression.

"Thank you for sharing with me," she whispered. "Can't imagine how difficult it must be to have a twin who is actually an older brother and to be in the family business with him."

He gave the bruise on her chin a tender kiss. "Mind if we change the subject?"

"I don't mind. Tell me something you like to do."

"I like creating new ideas, new products, being a development guy rather than a supervisor or a manager. Also, I'm always on the lookout for sideline business opportunities."

"New products are critical to the success of the business."

"I'm learning to like being on the receiving end of the respect and admiration Murphy usually gets."

"You've earned it. And you'll be a hero after we uncover the turncoat. So let's make sure you continue to get all the admiration and respect you can handle."

Chapter Sixteen

Annalisa opened her eyes to find Murdoch, dressed in only his black boxer briefs, sitting cross-legged on an overstuffed chair beside the chest of drawers. "Morning," she said, pulling the covers up under her chin.

"Good morning," he said with a smile. "Coffee?"

"I'd love some. Also, I keep forgetting to get a new phone. What time are you showing me your pillow talk secret? Should we shop before or after?"

"Let's eat, check in with Vic by teleconference, go to the village for your phone, and groceries, stop by Chief O'Malley's. Then we'll come back here for the secret."

"You're really organized for someone who only got about two hours sleep last night."

He ducked his head, looking sheepish. "Remember what we were doing all night, when we weren't sleeping?"

"Vividly."

"I'm ultra-organized this morning so we'll have

time to take a nap and do it again."

"Then I'd better shower." She started to throw off the covers, hesitated. "Where did my new clothes end up?"

"I brought everything up here," he said, pointing to stacks of jeans, sweaters, t-shirts, and a neat pile of underwear on the dresser. "Just in case."

"In case I agree to sleep with you in your room until I have to go home?"

Eyes wide, he looked stricken. "Home?"

She wasn't ready to revisit this topic, not until she knew she'd be able to make a lateral transfer from California. And she desperately needed clarification on Murdoch's mate deal. Besides, they had such an exciting, productive day ahead. Could she reassure Murdoch without making promises she couldn't keep? *Sure, just watch what you say.*

Annalisa threw back the covers, took a running step and launched herself at Murdoch. He caught her but overbalanced and together they tumbled backward out of the chair. Arms tight around her, he twisted in mid-fall. *Impossible.* No one was that flexible.

However it happened, he hit the floor first and she landed on top of him.

"Are you okay?"

"I'm peachy," she said, beginning to giggle. "You're the one who smacked the floor. How's your head?"

"Too thick to worry about," he said with a laugh.

After a good chuckle and a warm kiss, she traced the dragon tattoo on his chest. "Is there a story behind this?"

"There is. How about I tell you later, during our nap?"

"Ooh la la," she said jumping to her feet, "a sexy story."

When he grabbed for her ankle, she dodged away and ran for the bathroom. "Don't forget my coffee."

After her shower, Annalisa dressed in one of her new matching bra and pantie sets, new socks, new jeans, a new sweater and her old shoes. As she braided her hair, she warned her reflection, "Don't even think about more shopping. You're the spoiled one."

"Annalisa?"

She glanced around. It was Ryan's voice…on the intercom? "Hello?"

"I can't hear you, Murdoch silenced the bedroom mics. If you can hear me, press talk on the unit beside the bathroom door or the bedroom door."

She pressed, "Hello Ryan. What's up? *Over*."

Ryan laughed. "No need to say *over*, just release

the button to listen. Murdoch arranged breakfast and the teleconference with Vic in the secure room. Remember the way? Or do you need someone to come get you?"

She pressed, "I know the way. How much time do I have?"

"Could you meet us down there in fifteen minutes?"

She looked at her naked face and wished for thirty. "Roger, ten minutes, Over and out."

In the secure room, Annalisa forked an oversized bite of eggs Benedict into her mouth when the sleek Vic appeared on the big screen. "Bad news," Vic announced. "I heard from our traitor an hour ago. I was so close to pinpointing the location he was sending from, I delayed calling you."

"Understandable," Murdoch said. "Tell us the news."

Vic looked straight into her camera. "He's decided to hold an auction."

"Son of a bitch," Murdoch hissed.

"Shit," Ryan said under his breath.

"Which means we've lost control?" she asked.

"Exactly right," Vic said with a weak smile.

"How long do we have?" Murdoch asked.

"Forty-eight hours." Vic looked sick. "I can call in

a couple more people."

"How close are you, Vic?"

"Thirty minutes ago, I thought I had him. It could happen any time, but no more than twenty-four hours."

"Then keep going by yourself. If any of this leaks out, the publicity will kill us." Murdoch cleared his throat. "Do you need anything from us?"

"It's no longer simply a matter of money changing hands. The bastard is going to announce to selected buyers that our protocols are for sale. When...*when* I locate him, we need the Feds to act immediately on our information."

"I'll make those arrangements," Murdoch said. "Then, the timing gets even tighter. As soon as the Feds make a move, we need to recover our property, and make what amounts to a simultaneous announcement to the press. All a hoax, false alarm, nothing to see here. Muirdris Shipping isn't missing a damn thing."

"That'll be you again, Murdoch," Ryan said. "Why don't you let me and a couple of the guys handle the recovery? I'll contact you the instant I have our property in my hand."

"Thanks Ryan. Pick your team and tell me if you need anything," Murdoch said. "I'll be ready to face the press."

"Excuse me?" Annalisa spoke up. Murdoch nodded to her. "Sounds like location and communications are critical. Murdoch and I will be attending the ship christening late this afternoon followed by the ball tonight. I'm getting a smart phone today and will text each of you to confirm numbers. Murdoch will be carrying both his satellite and smart phone. Or have them close by."

"Thanks everyone and good luck to us," Murdoch said. He stood, lifted Annalisa to her feet and hugged her so tight it almost hurt.

The shopping trip to the village went like clockwork. Annalisa was setting up her new phone while Murdoch pushed a shopping cart through the grocery store.

Last stop was the check in with Chief O'Malley. He met them at the door to the police station. "Comeon back to my office. I've got bad news."

"Shit." Murdoch said under his breath. "Chief, this isn't the first bad news we've had today. Any reason my head of security, Ryan can't join us right now?"

"Bring him in. I know Ryan. Good man to have in a pinch."

Murdoch turned, went back outside to the Escalade, and invited Ryan to join them. "Chief said bad news. That's all I know."

"Damn."

"Agreed."

Seated in metal folding chairs around a scratched oak desk, in an office that smelled of burnt coffee, they waited for the Police Chief to speak.

"I talked to the State police. They ID'd the guy we took into in custody. He's a mental patient from New York. He was locked-down in the rehab facility when the truck was heisted."

"Just terrific," Ryan mumbled. He dropped his chin and rubbed the back of his neck.

"So," the chief said needlessly, "Our guy couldn't have stolen the truck or rear-ended Annalisa's rental car. He certainly couldn't've planted the car bomb in the Muirdris parking garage."

"Bottom line," Murdoch said quietly, "If the man who rear-ended Annalisa's car is still at large, then Annalisa is still in danger."

Chapter Seventeen

The silence in the Escalade during the ride back to Murdoch's house was oppressive. All the human tensions crammed into the enclosed space, combined with Murdoch's own apprehension, had his dragon pacing like a tiger in a zoo. Murdoch kept sensing someone was following them. And dismissed the notion. It hadn't originated from a legitimate dragon-instinct, but because he was suffering from a bad case of jitters. He'd gone back to fearing for Annalisa's safety.

His beast, on the other hand, claimed to *know* that someone, or something, was watching them. Again, Murdoch scoffed. Normally, the dragon's insight into the location and movements of enemies was extremely reliable, but in this atmosphere?

He took a deep breath. They'd all be much calmer once everyone was safely back inside his property. *Our Lair,* the dragon corrected.

Murdoch swallowed a snort. Now there's an out-of-date term. Anyway, it was time to reveal his dragon to his mate. No pressure. Only his future happiness hinged on her reaction, her acceptance. The dragon was fully committed. Murdoch hated to imagine his reaction if Annalisa was afraid of the beast. Or simply rejected him. There'd be hell to pay.

No backing out now, the arrangements had been made. Shifting into his sea dragon form took a lot of space and demanded privacy.

As the Escalade drove through the opening gate, Ryan signaled to the guard on duty.

"Ryan," Murdoch said, "are the arrangements all set for our security staff to meet at Murphy's estate?"

"Yes, sir. Per your instructions, that's the last man here. As he leaves, he'll set everything on your property to automatic for the next three hours. But under the circumstances, I can have him call all the men back, have them here in—"

"No, not yet. Let's stick with the plan. Park by the door, and check that your man is gone. I need to speak with Annalisa inside, and in private. To share something top secret. After she and I talk, I'll text you to join us. I've decided I want you to know as well."

"Thank you, Murdoch," Ryan said as the car stopped by the front steps. He turned back to look at Murdoch. "I appreciate the vote of confidence. And whatever it is, my lips are sealed."

His dragon stopped pacing. *Ryan knows.*

Suspects, maybe. But he will know in a short time.

Annalisa glanced back and forth between him and Ryan. During the pause, she took his hand.

Murdoch continued, "I've allowed time for questions, if you have any." *That was a joke. Of course, they'd have questions.* "Also, I want to take Annalisa down by the dock, show her the cliffs and the house from below. While we're there, I need you to keep watch for any boats approaching."

"I will, boss."

"While we're on the dock, call the men back. I want two full shifts of guards here when we get back upstairs. And for the foreseeable future. At time and a half pay."

"Are you still going to the shipyard?" Ryan asked.

"Absolutely," Murdoch said. *Oops.* He turned to his mate. "Sorry, I'm assuming again. Do you still…?"

"Absolutely," she said, imitating his tone. "And I think we should open the ball with a waltz and close it with a country line dance."

"You heard the lady, Ryan. Assign as many cars and bodyguards as you like, but we'll both be officiating at the ship's launch and tonight I'll be partying with the belle of the ball 'til they toss us out."

"Yes, boss."

The locks unclicked as he reached for the handle. "Stay here, Ryan, until we're inside. Then watch for my text."

He held the car door for Annalisa then hurried her inside the mansion. "Living room?"

"Kitchen."

He led the way to the spacious open kitchen beyond the dining room. They had several seating options. The central marble-topped island offered ten bar stools, or the smaller table in the breakfast nook boasted seating for six. And a bay window overlooking the coastline.

"By the window," she added.

He made sure she was comfortable, seated close enough that he could hold her hand, and then he blanked. She leaned forward, kissed him, squeezed his hand.

"Thanks," he breathed. "I don't know exactly how to tell you except to just come out with it. I was born a sea dragon shape shifter." He waited a moment for that to sink in.

"I have a human form—" he swept his hand down "—and I can shift into a large sea dragon. In that form, I look like a combination of sea serpent and dragon."

"Oh no, Murdoch. Seriously?" Her forehead

wrinkled with frown lines, she compressed her lips into a thin line. And she studied him. "Are you joking or—"

"It's okay," he reassured her. "I expected this reaction. Get your jacket back on. I'll text Ryan. We'll go out onto the side lawn and I'll show you."

He texted Ryan: "Bundle up. Meet us at the front door. Going to the side lawn for show and tell."

Turning back to his mate, he found her clutching the puffy outerwear, still staring.

"Hon," she whispered, "you aren't going to embarrass yourself in front of Ryan, are you?"

He wrestled the jacket from her grasp and dropped a peck on her lips. "I'd thank you for the *hon*, assuming it's short for *honey*, but I think it just slipped out. Now, put this on."

He shoved her arms into the empty sleeves and zipped the front closed. He grabbed her hand and towed her to the front entry. "Thank you, Sweetling, for worrying about my reputation." Hauling Annalisa against him, he kissed her hard, and she clung to him.

"Don't do this." Tears glistened on her eyelashes.

"Wipe your eyes," he admonished her. "You only have to trust me as far as the helipad."

"All right." Sniffing, she took his hand.

Between the front door and the fluttering wind-sock, he repeated his announcement to Ryan, and added, "For obvious reasons, I need to swear you to secrecy."

"Sea dragon or no sea dragon, I swear to you, word of honor, my lips are sealed."

"A diplomatic answer. Both of you stay here." He leaned to Annalisa and caressed his mate's cheek. "Remember, it's still me, breathing air, but I can't talk. If you want to touch me, that's fine, I can't hurt either of you. After I shift back, we'll go inside, and you can ask questions. Or have a stiff drink. Or both. Okay?"

Ryan nodded, and Annalisa blinked at him.

Jeez. He jogged from the edge of the helipad to the center of the broad expanse of snow covering the side lawn. Giving himself plenty of room, he called the dragon, who was prancing with excitement to meet their mate. "Steady, big guy."

The air around him shimmered and the next instant, he stood on four huge clawed feet, his relatively short wings spread wide and his mouth purposely closed over rows of long, sharp teeth. He angled his head and spotted Ryan and his mate, both wide-eyed but slowly walking toward him.

She knows us. The dragon carefully lowered his head to bring his eyes closer to hers. *Watch the tail,*

Murdoch warned his beast. The sea serpent part of their anatomy was mostly located aft, where he sported an extremely long tail ending in a wicked sharp barb as tall as Ryan.

I'd never hurt her.

"I know. Try to look cuddly."

Annalisa stopped right beside his jaw and looked into his eye. He tried a wink. She seemed to understand. "Murdoch?" she whispered, "Is it really you?"

His head moved slowly up and down. "Oh my God. Your scales are so beautiful. Look how they glint in the sunlight. And all the different shades of green. May I touch?"

Another nod. Without hesitation, she stepped forward, stroked her open hand across the scales beneath his eye. "They're smooth." She side-stepped to stroke his neck. The dragon vibrated with joy.

"Ryan," she called over her shoulder, "come here, you have to feel this. Oh, I think he's purring." She moved on to touch his leathery wings and stare down at the short legs and oversized feet and claws.

Ryan touched with his fingertips only. "Damned impressive, boss. This is some wicked awesome secret."

"I'm going to avoid that tail," Annalisa said as she

returned to his head. "Besides, I have a million questions. If we go back to the helipad can you become Murdoch again?"

The dragon balked.

"Just for questions," Murdoch soothed. "Then we show her the hoard." In an instant, the dragon was curled up inside and Murdoch stood, fully clothed, on a massive, sea-dragon-shaped expanse of melted snow.

Inside, he guided his mate and new best friend to the library. "If you'll light the fire, Ryan, I'll make us Irish coffees."

"Plain coffee for me," Ryan said from beside the hearth. "I'm on duty. And um…recovering."

"Good on you." *Damn, it was a day for coming out.*

"I'll take Ryan's portion of Bailey's." Annalisa glanced at the man lighting kindling. "It if won't bother—"

"Not at all." Ryan assured them. Snagging his coffee mug, Ryan settled in a chair across from where he and Annalisa sat on the loveseat.

"Cozy," Murdoch said. "Let me start with a wee bit of clan history. Our family started as purebred dragons, in Ireland during the time of the druids. But through the centuries, the number of females dwindled. When an ancestor approached another clan, a group of fire-breathers, about finding mates, he and the entire delegation were blindsided and murdered."

He took a sip of the coffee and said a silent prayer of remembrance for his ancestors. "The surviving males of the clan decided to cautiously look elsewhere. After hearing of a clan of sea serpents with the opposite problem, too many females and a worry about interbreeding, a new delegation went on a specific search. Legend has it that every meeting produced fated mates. The couples recognized each other as mates, which made all the couplings happy occasions. And it only took one generation to produce hybrids like Mu...uh, me."

"Identical twins." Ryan said. "Murphy must be a sea dragon, too."

"Never ask," Murdoch warned. "It's his choice to tell or not."

Ryan raised his right hand, like he was being sworn in. "On threat of death."

Chapter Eighteen

Annalisa enjoyed watching Murdoch and Ryan interact. Their friendship seemed to deepen every minute they were together. It had certainly expanded earlier when each man—well, one man, one sea dragon shifter—shared his most closely guarded secret. Murdoch apparently trusted Ryan to keep quiet about both his and Murphy's hidden natures.

Did mates have greater access to sea dragon mysteries than friends? Did she want access? She was getting in deeper and deeper here. Murdoch continued to call her Sweetling and referred to her as his mate. What would happen if she decided to return to California? Go home to her life, and her job? Did the sea dragon shifter clan have mind wipe technology?

Annalisa rubbed her forehead trying for the spot where the headache throbbed. Murdoch took her hand and began to gently massage. Still chatting with Ryan about fighting techniques in sea dragon form, he applied pressure to the web between her thumb and index finger. Her headache retreated to the background.

Sitting up straighter, she silently reaffirmed her goals. She'd come a long way, been through a lot, and she wasn't going away until the Muirdris spy was identified and in custody. Meanwhile, she needed to pay closer attention to the information Murdoch was offering. On the wild chance she decided to become the mate of a billionaire sea dragon, she'd bet serious money there was a qualifying exam. Or at least an in-depth interview.

"Do you have to fight often?" she asked.

"No. There are almost no territorial disputes any more. We do have an annual obligation to provide protection. But it only requires one or two of us to go and in a defensive capacity only. I'm a full-time businessman."

"How do you breathe underwater?" Ryan asked.

"I control my body system that allows me to process oxygen like a fish or I can choose to function like a dolphin or whale, returning to the surface for air. In that configuration, I can hold my breath for almost fifteen minutes. But the change-over to gills is fast."

"The sea dragon clan picked the ideal business to go into," Ryan said. "You can observe and protect your ships and cargos from all angles."

"No comment," he responded.

"God," Ryan gasped. "I'm really sorry, Murdoch. Fuck, I didn't mean to—"

"Ryan, it's okay between us. But you need to keep a tight rein around anyone else."

"Maybe I should shut up now and—"

"No." Murdoch shook his head. "Let's get more of your questions answered." He smiled at Annalisa. "Next?"

"Can you fly?" she asked.

"Barely. I'm aquadynamic not aerodynamic. My body is way too long with not enough wing surface. I can shoot up out of the water and flap like crazy to reach a sand dune on shore. But most of the time I waddle ashore and shift right there."

"And you were dressed," she said. "How can you come back with all your clothes on?"

"Dragons are mythical creatures and all the ones I'm aware of, shift back with all their clothing intact."

"Handy," Ryan observed.

She silently agreed. In her favorite romance stories, the werewolves needed to plan ahead, big time. *Whoa*…were there… no, she'd ask that question when she had Murdoch alone.

"What about breathing fire?" she asked.

"Excellent question. No fire, but I can do damage

by power-blasting water from my mouth, like a fire hose."

"Got to assume," Ryan mused, "your best speed is submerged."

"You'd be correct." For the first time today, Murdoch's mischievous grin appeared. "You could say I'm wicked fast."

"Are you talking Marlin fast?" Ryan asked.

"Wait, you lost me," Annalisa said. "I thought sailfish were the fastest."

"Doesn't matter," Murdoch boasted, "I can beat them both. Maintain a speed in excess of a sailfish over a distance much longer than a Marlin."

"Ocean races?" she asked with a curl at the corner of her lip.

"Sweetling, I am a male."

After Ryan left to patrol the gates, she and Murdoch raided the refrigerator for a light lunch. "Do you trust me and the dragon enough to ride on him for thirty yards? I want to show you a big cavern in the cliffs but the only way in is to swim underwater."

"Like with SCUBA gear?"

"I have a wetsuit for you, tanks and all the equipment. But if you're up for it, I'd like to show you how safe and easy riding a sea dragon can be."

"Can we practice once or twice before we go into

an underwater tunnel?"

"Of course."

Over a grilled chicken salad and glass of milk, he drew a picture of his sea dragon's back on a sheet of paper. "Here's where the gills open. If you lay flat on my neck and hang on to these small side horns, your face will be right in the path of the backwash from the gills. It forms a stream of air and you can put your face in it and breathe. You'll know you've got the right spot because it replaces the water and feels like wind on your face. We'll practice on the surface until you're ready."

After lunch, she slid on a colorful wetsuit over her t-shirt and panties, and carrying goggles, she followed Murdoch out on the terrace off the living room.

"Okay, up on my back," he said. She looked at him, then peered over the edge of the railing. "How are we getting down to the water?"

"Jump," he said. "You may want to close your eyes for the split second while I shift but you won't fall. The updrafts are strong here, and we'll coast to the surface and land like an airplane."

Terror washed through her. Followed by a bolt of red-hot rage. "You are out of your fucking mind," she shrieked. "Let's review. I climb on your back. You jump off a multistory terrace. I close my eyes while you turn into a beautiful but scaly dragon. While we drop, I try to figure out where to hang on. The dragon flaps like crazy to keep us from plummeting into the sea. He and I die, splattered on the rocks below."

"You don't like my plan?"

"Not a plan. A double suicide. I fucking hate it."

"You're so cute when you talk dirty."

"Insane."

"You'd rather take the stairs?"

She whipped off the goggles and smacked him repeatedly all the way to the medieval staircase. She followed Murdoch down past the entrance to the secure room, through a thick, locked door, and they kept going down and around the stairs. Finally, Murdoch stopped. Through another locked door, the stairs ended in a long wooden landing, a dock? Water lapped against the far edge and a small boat bobbed to one side, tugging against its mooring.

Murdoch pressed a concealed control and the wall beyond the end of the dock rose like a garage door. Sunlight streamed in.

"No more teasing," he said. "It's important to me that we learn to swim together, and you have a good time. How about I swim out, shift and come back as close as I can to get you? You'll be in the cold water less than a minute. Or paddle out in the boat and climb aboard from there?"

"I'll jump in and climb aboard."

"What a woman." He kissed her, left both his phones on the bottom stair and dove off the end of the dock. A minute later, the sea dragon's head broke the surface of the water and slid toward the dock.

She let out a wolf whistle. Wet, his green scales shimmered like precious gems. She stayed on the end of the dock and when the dragon was still, she slipped into the freezing water and followed the heat. She recognized the small side-horn she'd been told to hang on to, used it to pull herself onto the dragon's neck. His body pumped heat, warming her and the water around him.

The first practice went perfectly. She breathed in air from his gills while warmed ocean water flowed over her body. When the dragon raised his head and brought them to the surface, she said, "Okay, let's go through the tunnel."

Excitement replaced fear. It was becoming an adventure. The tunnel was wider than she'd imagined, and shorter. In no time, they reached the other side and the dragon surfaced in a sparkling, glittering wonderland. She gasped, not knowing where to look first. He lumbered his enormous body onto a pile of gold coins, next to more piles of coins, loose gems, jewelry and what looked like over-flowing pirate chests.

She slid down his scales, landed on her feet and scrambled for distance until she remembered this was going the other way. She turned to find Murdoch standing on a pile of coins watching her.

"It's beyond amazing," she said. "Where'd it all come from?"

"Do you like it?" He opened his arms.

"It's unbelievable. Magnificent." She stumbled and slid toward him. Finally, she threw herself the last yard. Her arms wrapped around his neck, her legs circled his waist. Her fingers gripped his hair and hung on. The kiss was hot and deep. His tongue seduced hers and she moaned. He broke the kiss and moved his mouth to nibble on her earlobe while his talented fingers started to peel off the wetsuit.

"Wait, just a minute?" She wanted him but wanted a couple of answers too.

He jerked his head up, his brows knitted with concern.

"Murdoch. It was truly exciting swimming underwater on your dragon. And this place? It's beyond words. If you want us to make love here, I'd like that too. But first, please explain what all this is and what it means to you and to the dragon." She shivered with the realization of how little she knew about him.

He relaxed his shoulders. "I couldn't think how to explain it, especially after our misunderstandings about money. You're right. You need to know, deserve to understand what this means to me." He led her to a long flat chest, sat down on the closed lid, and pulled her onto his lap.

"All this is my main—sorry, *our*—main hoard. Collected over generations and passed down as dragons died. It's a tradition to show your mate the hoard and gift her with the most valuable pieces. In the old days, dragons draped their mates in as much of their hoard as she could wear."

"Wow."

"Right. Another expectation is that the mate will be overwhelmed and overjoyed by the size and value of the hoard." He made a subtle gesture indicating the dragon inside him. "And you, Annalisa, my Sweetling mate, just aced that one."

"Whew."

"I'd—we'd—be honored if you'd accept a piece of hoard jewelry and wear it. It doesn't have to be an engagement ring. Think of it as a promise ring, or a necklace, or a locket to show we're going steady."

"I'd be delighted. You choose the piece and we'll go steady, for the time being."

Murdoch stood and sat her on the chest. He selected a priceless antique necklace from an overflowing domed travelling trunk nearby. With great ceremony he draped the piece around her neck and fastened the gold clasp at the back of her neck.

"Now we get naked and celebrate?" she teased.

"Exactly."

Chapter Nineteen

Murdoch led his mate to a flat mossy area and, removing her wetsuit, he left it spread open beneath her while he took a minute to admire her beauty and all those voluptuous curves on display in her tight little muscle-shirt and bikini panties. Not only was she beautiful and desirable, the inner woman was phenomenal as well.

She'd made his heart stutter by agreeing to wear his hoard jewelry. The necklace glittered in the dim light and his breath caught at the sight. Here she was, almost naked, lying in the middle of his hoard and eager to make love with him.

Claim her.

We can't today. Too soon.

The dragon roared his anger. *Claim her now!*

We will. Soon.

The dragon howled his disappointment. Annalisa was the first human mate in the sea dragon clan's history, yet the beast had his facts correct, knew his lore.

If Murdoch used the condom he'd brought along, this wouldn't be a true claiming. For that, he needed to spill his seed inside his mate. And his heart told him she wasn't ready. And she certainly wasn't ready to risk getting pregnant.

If he assured her, she'd probably believe that as a mythical shifter he couldn't catch or spread any diseases. But without protection, he could very well impregnate her. And their offspring, male or female, would be born looking like a human baby but would also be a sea dragon shifter. A lot for a human woman to accept and adapt to.

Ask her.

Damn it. The dragon was persistent. *What the hell.* Since today had turned into a series of question and answer sessions, he'd at least explain the situation while he teased and pleasured his mate.

Stripping his clothes off, Murdoch grabbed a handful of loose gems, some random pieces of jewelry and stretched out beside her. He pulled off her t-shirt, propped himself on one elbow and arranged a circle of matching emeralds around each of her nipples.

"Can I bring you to a climax without knocking any of these off?"

She chuckled, and the motion sent three gems sliding off her breasts. "Oops."

"Hold still." He slowly bent over her, drawing out the anticipation. His tongue darted out and flicked one nipple. She gasped, and two more emeralds slid away.

He tried to look severe. "Concentrate."

"I am concentrating." She huffed, and all the remaining emeralds scattered. He swept the gems off her neck and abdomen, cupped one breast, working the nipple with his thumb while he suckled the other. Annalisa moaned. He kept worshiping her breasts, patiently alternating hand and mouth until she writhed.

He released the wet nipple and slowed his caressing hand. Looking into her eyes, he said, "Annalisa Bartello, my dragon and I recognized you immediately as our fated life mate. That means, I will love you, unconditionally and completely, for the rest of my rather long life. No matter if you accept me as your mate or not. I'm committed to protecting you with my own life, providing for you with all that I possess, and showering you with my hoard. Again, it makes no difference what your commitment level is. I know this sounds intense. But it in no way translates to any form of stalking."

"Actually, that's a lovely declaration."

"It's the absolute truth. Remember, just this morning you had no idea sea dragon shifters existed. Not only do they exist, but one of them is in a lifelong committed relationship with you. When mates are two dragons, they can feel the immediate strong attraction and know what it is. I'm not sure if it's the same with a human and a dragon. Have you wondered what you're feeling?"

Annalisa shoved at his chest and he instantly moved back to give her room. Rolling to her feet, she marched away from him. When she stepped on loose coins, she stumbled. With a disgusted humph, she plopped down on the pile of gold, her back to him.

"I think I feel it too, Murdoch. But it's such a crazy idea—love at first sight is stupid—so I'd accepted the physical attraction while trying to ignore the emotional pull." She swung her legs around to face him, brushing stuck coins off her legs.

"The truth is, I do love you," she admitted, "and want to live with you forever. When I'm with you, I'm certain I can manage both my job and this relationship. With our combined strength, I just know I can have both. Same with kids. Never did I dream I'd want to start a family right away. But together, you and I can handle it."

She wrinkled her nose. "No, it's much more than that. I know in my heart, we will be together forever, and we'll thrive and laugh and love."

Murdoch ears rang, and his heart hammered in his chest. *She loves us.*

You were right, big guy. Where's the ring?

He palmed the diamond ring from the same chest as the necklace and dropped to his knees in front of Annalisa. "I love you and want us to be together for eternity. For you to be the mother of our children. Will you marry me?"

"Yes. I'll marry you." He slid the glittering diamond solitaire on her finger. An exact fit. Then he swept her into his arms and returned her to their wet-suit-nest. He kissed her, tried to show her what she meant to him. When they came up for air, he cupped her face in his hands and said, "About baby shifters…"

"Oh, I'm on birth control, so if you're healthy… Sorry, guess that's a silly question."

He stroked his thumbs across her cheeks and explained about shifter health.

"I've never had unprotected sex," she said, slipping off her panties.

"Let's find out how it feels."

He slowly worked his way from ravaging her mouth, to kissing and licking most of her body. She screamed with the first orgasm atop his hoard while his head was buried between her thighs. Before she'd recovered, he urged Annalisa up on her hands and knees and slid into her slick hot pussy from behind. Her tight muscles enveloped him. The sensation was so intense he almost lost it right then.

He set a varied pace, thrusting in quickly then slowly pulling out until only the head of his cock remained. Another advantage of this position, both his hands were available. He stroked and fondled her nipples, then her back and her sweet butt.

When she gasped a demand for, "Faster. Harder." he obliged. And when his fingertips touched her clit, she exploded again.

His cock felt every pulse, each squeeze and spasm as her body urged him to follow. He thrust deeper. Then, with a wild cry, he emptied into her.

Positioning Annalisa on top of him, he envisioned their babies as he stroked her hair. "No pillows," he grumbled.

"We don't need them," she said. "Tell me another secret."

"I call this my main hoard because I have more."

"This fixation on wealth, it's a dragon thing, right?"

"'Fraid so."

She lifted her head and rolled her eyes at him.

An hour later, they swam back to the hidden

dock, Murdoch retrieved his phones—one missed call from Ryan—and they climbed up the staircase together.

He pressed recall. "Hey Ryan, We're back in the house. Everything okay?"

"We need to discuss a departure time. The traffic toward the shipyards is messed up. We'll need to leave earlier."

"Meet us in the library and bring your best estimate of the travel time."

Annalisa, back in jeans and a t-shirt, sank onto the couch, while he stood with Ryan beside the dying fire.

"Too bad the helicopter isn't here."

"Agreed," Murdoch said, then shrugged. No way would his Annalisa agree to the expense of a last minute, chartered helicopter. Proving once again she was the perfect mate for a frugal dragon.

"Everyone will expect you to drive?" Annalisa asked from across the room.

"Yes," Ryan answered. "Especially with Murphy out of town. When the Jetstream goes overseas, the helicopter stays parked at Logan airport, so Murphy can arrive back anytime he wants to and have a ride home."

"So..." she said in a slow voice, "how much is it...no wait, that's not what I want to ask. Compared to doing exactly what the bad guy is expecting us to do, how risky is it to charter a helicopter, fly the three or 4 of us to the shipyard and then to the roof of the hotel where the ball is being held?"

Murdoch gave Ryan a nod. "This is your question, security expert."

Ryan smiled. "The flight from here to the shipyards is as safe as anyone could hope for. Even me. Once we arrive by air, the risk on the hotel leg increases a little. The last leg, from the roof of the hotel back to here? That becomes the most dangerous. But again, unless the bad guy has a commando unit or several rocket launchers? Minimal risk."

Annalisa nodded slowly. "Then I vote we go with the safest plan. Let's fly."

Murdoch grinned at Ryan. "Make it so."

This time Annalisa's eye roll was epic.

Chapter Twenty

A nervous shiver ran up her spine as Annalisa dressed for the ship christening in the one business suit she'd packed, and Bridget had managed to save. *A helicopter was picking them up.* She'd never flown in one before. She zipped closed her overnight bag with new dress jeans and California State University at Long Beach sweatshirt for the ball. Certainly not a losing sports program, CSULB was her alma mater. The sweatshirt was the other major survivor of the crushed suitcase.

She glanced down at her left hand for the umpteenth time since Murdoch had put the ring on her finger. Once again, the oversized diamond winked back at her. The flashy ring was so Murdoch. A wave of heat and love washed through her. And she was never taking it off.

The chopper ride—now she understood the nickname—was scary, noisy, and fun. Another new fact, when you arrived at a shipyard function in a helicopter, it attracted lots of attention. The press, TV cameras, a cluster of Muirdris execs and yelling paparazzi rushed over to them.

Ryan trotted ahead, swearing and barking orders into his phone.

Murdoch smiled and waved to everyone. Before she could turn the ring on her finger to hide the stone, Murdoch put his arm around her in a move more effective than a bullhorn announcement. Flash units on every camera exploded with blinding light.

Athletic looking people in dark suits and wearing ear-pods, hurried over to escorted them to the VIP box, situated front and center in the VIP section of the stands.

She tried to take her seat between Vic and Murdoch, but *her fiancé* decided to introduce her, one by one, to every person in the box. Some kind soul shoved a glass of cold Coke into her grasp. Between handshakes, she took a quick swallow and the lady talking to her stopped in mid-sentence to gape at the diamond in her ring.

Vic touched Murdoch's elbow. "They're starting," she whispered and escorted them back to their seats.

To kick off the ceremonies, Murdoch went down to the microphone to give a short speech. He stressed the eco advantages of this new ship and reaffirmed Muirdris Shipping's commitment to bringing all their container carriers up to the higher standard.

As his speech ended, a woman in a Muirdris security uniform signaled to Ryan, who was standing just behind Murdoch. Ryan nodded, returned Murdoch to the box, and hurried back to the woman. Annalisa only heard pieces of the next speech. Where was Ryan?

Murdoch's smartphone vibrated in his pocket. He bent his head forward and toward her, angling the phone she could hear the conversation. "Mr. Rudraige? Alice Washburn, security. We've got a problem and Ryan instructed me to call you. My supervisor told me it was nothing to worry about, so I reported it to Ryan, right after your speech."

"What's the problem?"

"I noticed a man in an overcoat who appears to be wearing a wetsuit underneath. He's lugging a soft-sided briefcase, and whatever's in there, it's heavy."

"Do we have metal scanners?"

"Yes, sir, at all entrances. I don't believe he carried that case in today."

"Where did Ryan go?"

"Looking for the man on the next dock. Ryan told me to alert you, then call for back up."

"Good job, Alice. My orders are: give me ten minutes, then call in the cavalry."

Murdoch hung up and spoke into directly into Annalisa's ear. "I'm going after Ryan. Next dock. Please stay here. Swear, I'll call. Love you."

She gave a quick nod and pulled out her phone. Gripping it, she watched Murdoch's back until he turned a corner.

*   *   *

Murdoch

When he was out of sight of the reviewing stands, Murdoch broke into a run. He called the dragon, just short of an actual shift, to search the air and the surface of the docks for any trace of Ryan.

Been here. Not now.

Talk about cryptic. A more detailed answer would help. Halfway down the dock, the dragon heard a groan. Ryan?

Yes. Hurt.

Murdoch sped up, pounding toward the cluster of small temporary structures at the end of the dock.

Blood.

Shit. Despite the warning, he almost tripped over

Ryan. His security chief was sitting on the dirty surface of the dock, slumped against a metal storage building. His overcoat was nowhere in sight, his suit jacket half on and half off. The white dress shirt was bloody, the right sleeve torn off and tied around a wound on Ryan's upper arm.

"Need an ambulance?" Murdoch asked as he crouched to get a better look at Ryan's face.

"Hell no," Ryan grunted. "I'm good, just woozy. Bleeding's stopped. Briefcase guy's partner jumped me, then the bastard ran." He struggled to his feet, leaned against the metal siding, and pointed to the end of the dock. "Briefcase guy went into the water off the end of this dock carrying a heavy payload."

Murdoch pulled off his overcoat and wrapped it around Ryan. "You suspect a bomb?"

"I'd say a bomb like the one at headquarters. What we need now is some serious muscle under water."

"At your service." Murdoch handed Ryan his phone and took off, running flat out. When he dove off the end of the dock, he told the dragon, "All yours."

He shifted after he was completely hidden beneath the dark water. With a whip of his tail, he shot through the water separating the two docks. Racing along the length of the massive vessel, he looked for any signs of a diver, or anything attached to the hull. Zip.

He slipped under the propellers to check the other side. *There.* The dragon roared his challenge. The bomber turned, started, and dropped something. The explosive device stayed attached to the hull.

Bad. Danger, the dragon insisted.

Go get it, big guy.

The bomber froze, screaming under his mask, too terrified to swim away. The dragon gave a tail-pump and rolled to his side as he approached the bomb. He snagged it with two claws, then chewed it into little pieces with enormous teeth set in his powerful jaws. Explosive parts drifted down through the murky water.

The dragon turned his attention to the *bad man*.

But the man had torn off his mask and breathing equipment. In his panic, he'd drowned rather than go to the surface.

Dead.

Buck up, big guy. You got to chew the bomb. Forget the man.

The dragon pouted but obeyed. He swam to the end of the new ship's dock and made a mid-leap shift.

When Murdoch climbed the rest of the way up the ladder, only his shoes and socks were wet. And hey, good timing, they were still making speeches. He hurried to the stands and slipped into his seat as the automatic champagne bottle struck the bow of the ship, cracked open, and sprayed bubbly wine.

After the crowds began to thin, Ryan handed back Murdoch's phone and insisted on returning the coat.

"Only," Murdoch told him, "if you get that arm checked over at the onsite medi-center. We'll wait for you. I know you'll want to hear all about our adventures. And ask somebody to bring you a clean shirt."

"I'm wearing black tie," Ryan said. "Monkey suit is on the chopper."

"No prize money for you."

Before he'd leave, Ryan assigned three body-guards to protect Vic, Annalisa and Murdoch while they waited for him.

"I suppose I'll be billed for this, too," Murdoch grumbled. It seemed worth it when his mate hugged him and whispered in his ear, "My hero."

Ryan and Alice returned together. "I got him," Alice announced with obvious pride. "Not the briefcase guy but his partner. The one who sliced Ryan."

"Good work, Alice," Murdoch said.

"Turned him over to the police. And we have divers down now making sure the briefcase man didn't leave a bomb. I'll call Ryan if we learn anything more tonight."

On the helicopter flight to the hotel, Murdoch tried to tell his friends and mate all about the dragon's underwater adventure without yelling.

"He chewed up the bomb, ripped it apart. The bomber saw the beast tearing into his bomb and panicked. The dragon was going to force him to the surface, to surrender to the authorities, but the idiot was screaming, tore off his mask and drowned. The dragon left the body down there."

Annalisa made a *tisk* sound. "It's a miracle we weren't all blown to bits."

Murdoch shrugged. "The dragon never claimed to be a bomb expert. Bite, rip and claw, that's his style."

Ryan leaned over to Vic, and asked "You already knew about the boss?"

Vic gave him a vague shrug. The two of them stared at each other.

Chapter Twenty-One

Sliding his arm around his mate, Murdoch gave up trying to talk over the helicopter's rotor noise. Instead, he gazed out of his window, watching the lights below change as they flew over towns, villages, highways.

Once the authorities established that the man who'd drowned trying to bomb Muirdris's newest vessel was the same man who'd succeeded in bombing the parking garage, the direct attack on Muirdris Shipping was over. The dragon did his thing, and that threat was stopped. With the bomber's partner in custody, they might even get some answers. Like "why?"

He pulled Annalisa closer. Kudos to the beast, but Murdoch's mission was still in limbo. He had yet to prove himself. His mate had travelled all the way from California to warn him of a potentially devastating electronic threat to Muirdris. One that would have international consequences and affect the entire clan. And he'd accepted the challenge to finally prove to Murphy and the other directors that he was worthy.

So far, the jury was still out.

He needed to think of a way to identify the person who'd sent the emails offering to sell Muirdris port secrets. According to Vic, she was close, but she kept hitting cyber walls. Was there a way to get around those? He couldn't discuss it here, in mid-flight. He'd pull Vic aside for a private conversation as soon as they landed. They could find a quiet corner in the Muirdris VIP suite provided by the hotel for the four of them to freshen up and dress for the ball.

The chopper landing, setting down on the hotel's roof helipad, was obviously a thrill for his mate. He held Annalisa's hand as she stepped off the helicopter and automatically ducked. He led her out of range of the blades and pointed out the 365-degree view of the lights of Boston and the harbor. During their long, deep kiss, he made a silent pledge to her.

I swear, I'll figure out the emails and stop this guy.

The hotel manager came forward, with two bellpeople in tow. The silver-haired man introduced himself and greeted each new arrival with a firm handshake. The garment bags and small suitcases were whisked away.

In the service elevator, Murdoch caught Vic's eye. "You brought your computer?"

"Always."

"Sweetling?" he turned to Annalisa, "I need a few minutes with Vic. There are two master bedrooms with baths in the suite. Could you — ?"

"No problem," his gorgeous mate said. "I'll go first. I need more one-on-one time with the blow-dryer."

"Sure, boss." Ryan agreed. "But as soon as I'm dressed, I want to check out security in the ballroom. I'll assign one of our people at the door of the suite until I return."

Inside the spacious apartment, Murdoch made sure Annalisa had everything she needed and then stepped back into the living room. Vic was sitting at the desk, her computer open in front of her. She glanced up and said, "Cool. I recognize that expression. You have a new idea."

He sat beside her and explained his plan to avoid the next cyber wall. "I'm thinking once you established your fake ID and responded to the original email, they were able to program sender-specific walls. Let's try snooping from a whole new server *and* use an under-the-wall approach."

She sat motionless for a moment. Then Vic's eye grew wide and a broad smile lit up the sharp features of her face. "That combo might just work."

He moved to the picture window, giving her

room to work. When Ryan, resplendent in a custom tuxedo, cautiously opened his bedroom door, Murdoch waved him forward. Ryan tiptoed through the living room and surreptitiously exited the suite. Vic, her fingers dancing over the keyboard, never looked up.

A few moments later, Vic jerked back, her hands gripping the lip of the desk so hard her knuckles turned white.

"Don't shift," he ordered. "Do. Not. Shift." Murdoch's dragon-alpha-voice commanded.

"Son of a bitch," she hissed, panting hard.

"Maintain," he said, adding, "I need you to tell me what you found."

Her fox claws retracted into furry paws. The paws transformed into long-fingered human hands. Vic released her grip on the desk. "Sorry."

"Stop apologizing and tell me. Who is it?"

"Darren Weaton. My executive assistant. One of my team is offering top secret Muirdris port protocols for sale to the highest bidder. Oh, Mr. Rudraige, how can I ever…"

"Vic, stop right now. Mr. Rudraige? You haven't called me that in a decade. You can have your first-ever breakdown later. First, we need to figure out how Darren got his hands on the protocols. Who gave them to him or gave him access? Then—"

"Wait. Now that I know it's Darren, I'll search all his accounts, find out when and how he got the secret data." Her fingers started typing on the keyboard while she spoke.

"Should we confront him here?" Murdoch asked "Tonight? The sooner the better—right?"

"In terms of stopping the auction and releasing an immediate corporate denial, yes. Absolutely, the sooner the better. But how to manage the timing and avoid negative publicity? That's Ryan's call."

When all four of them were dressed, he stood beside Annalisa in his jeans and an MIT sweatshirt, and Vic announced, "Darren didn't have an accomplice. Thanks to my brilliant training and mentorship, he was able to hack into the protocols. I slammed an electronic lid on that shit, and reprogramed. Hell, I even changed the passcodes."

"Not your fault," Ryan whispered to her. "We'll take Darren down late tonight. Hustle him out of the hotel and into lockdown. Right now, it's time to get you and that hot dress out on the dancefloor." He gave Vic, sexy in a tight-fitting beaded ball gown, a hungry look.

*   *   *

Annalisa

Annalisa's knees quaked when the orchestra played the first strains of a waltz and Murdoch rose to his feet, extending his hand to her. "Our dance," he said.

She eyed the empty floor, noting all eyes were on Murdoch. "Alone?"

"I'll be with you."

With a steadying breath, she stood, and he escorted her to the middle of the room. Fighting the urge to look down at his feet, she gave him a wan smile and clung to his hand, a tight grip on his shoulder. He started slow, used both his hands to telegraph his next move. Pretty soon they were moving around the center of the floor like old pros. Well, he danced like a professional, and made her look good.

When the music stopped, applause filled the room. Then other couples streamed onto the dancefloor. She raised questioning brows at Murdoch.

"Another waltz," he said. "Might as well stick with what we know works."

"Oh really? How could you be sure we—"

"Let's try covering a little more territory. We'll add the progressive basic."

"The what?"

"Relax. Just the opposite of the box we've been

doing. I'll lead." He placed his arm and palm on her upper back and guided her in time to the music.

With the new pattern they worked their way to the outer perimeter and joined several experienced couples circling the floor. "Now, I'm going to exaggerate our turns," he whispered. "No new steps, just wider."

"Okay." After a few turns they'd covered serious ground. "This is fun," she confided.

"Start saving up for a floor length gown."

"They look wonderful twirling."

"And people can't see you stepping on my toes."

At the midpoint of the event, the caterer set out an elaborate buffet. The centerpiece was an ice carving of the new ship complete with stacked shipping containers from around the world.

At a signal from the head waiter, Murdoch stood "Gotta lead the way. Can I get you ladies plates, or would you rather come along and select for yourselves?"

"I'm going to powder my nose," Vic said. "Ryan, I'm counting on you to bring back red meat." Ryan snapped a salute.

"I'm with Vic," Annalisa announced. "And I'll eat anything, thanks."

Giddy with the excitement of dancing with Murdoch and the splendor of the ball, she followed Vic, seemingly an expert at weaving her way through a crowd. They exited the ballroom and strode down the hall.

As they approached the entrance, Vic literally ran into a dark-haired young man in a tux. "Darren," she gasped, a mixture of revulsion and fear on her face.

Annalisa moved forward to stand beside her. This was Vic's personal assistant. The one she'd avoided on her visit to Muirdris headquarters. She'd overheard him talking to Ji but never got a good look at his face.

Here, Darren's expressive face told its own story. His surprise turned to shock and then morphed into pure hatred. Annalisa almost stepped back again, but Vic held her ground, so she did too. Darren jutted his red face closer.

"So, you finally figured it out?" he spat. "You act so smart, so superior to the rest of us, but you're nothing more than a stupid, over-paid bitch."

"What—" Annalisa began.

"Darren is the one auctioning off Muirdris secrets," Vic said in an undertone.

"And," he snarled, "we can't have either one of you repeating that bit of information." He pulled a deadly looking gun from under his tux jacket. "Move, now. Past the restrooms, into the supply closet."

The sign on the door read: 'Authorized employees only' but the door was unlocked. Inside, floor to ceiling shelves were loaded with bathroom supplies and hotel equipment. Near the back corner, a pipe ran floor to ceiling

"I plan for every contingency," he said. Standing them beside the pipe, he zip-tied their hands behind their backs, and around the pipe. Shoving them down to sit on the tile floor, he tied their ankles with extension cords.

Shaking out linen napkins, he fashioned gags. "One more box to check, then I'll be back. What'll it be, whores? Death by stabbing? I have a butcher knife. Or should I bring the sound suppresser for this gun?"

Re-holstering the weapon, he peeked out into the hallway. "All clear. While I'm gone, you two take a vote. Decide how you want to die."

Chapter Twenty-Two

The lock on the storage closet door clicked. Annalisa closed her eyes and dug deep for a memory. Last year, in a weak moment of tipsy bravado, three of her beach volleyball buddies had challenged the remaining three to a timed contest, escaping from zip-ties. Based solely on U-tube videos, the challengers swore it could be done. She remembered some of the steps and a big caution. It didn't work on ties designed to tighten with pressure.

"Don't worry, it'll be okay," a soft voice said beside her. Vic? Annalisa's eyes flew open. Vic gave her a toothy grin, the napkin gag shredded in her lap.

"Hough loo uh at?"

Vic smiled. "Hold still and I'll get your gag off, with my teeth."

Her teeth? She stared down at the shredded napkin.

"Hold still," Vic said, "and trust me."

Annalisa froze and closed her eyes for good measure. The knot at the back of her neck released. Her napkin, now with several puncture marks, settled on the front of her sweatshirt.

"Thank you, much better," Annalisa said, licking her lips. "I think I remember how to get out of zip-ties. Let me try it for a few seconds. If it doesn't work, be thinking how to at least get the electric cords untied." She began moving her hands behind her back.

"I need to tell you something," Vic said, "in case it might help in planning our escape."

"I'll keep working on my ties. You talk."

"Um, I'm an Arctic fox. I bit—"

"Oh my God," Annalisa breathed, "that's wonderful. You can rescue us."

"No, sadly, I can't. Not the way the bastard has us positioned. Annalisa, keep working on your restraints while I explain what I can and can't do. I can call on my fox's teeth and strength to chew off napkins. I could chew through the electric wire if either one of us was a contortionist and could get her ankles to my mouth. Same with the zip ties. I can't get to them and besides, I suspect that result would be bloody. Our number one priority and our biggest obstacles are the ties and the pipe. Also, I can't fully shift with my hands tied around a pipe."

"And you'd ruin that dress."

"You're becoming an expert on shifter lore. Naked and dress replacement are the least of our worries. How are you doing back there?"

"I'm remembering the technique. How much time do you think we have?"

"We can't even guess without knowing what Darren considers his final box to be checked." She growled low in her throat. "If I could get my teeth into that damned —"

"Let me describe what I'm doing," Annalisa interrupted. "Get you started."

She described the technique to Vic and continued with her moves. "When we get loose, should we pound on the door? To attract attention? Or should we arm ourselves, wait for Darren, and beat the shit out of him with a surprise attack?"

"Excellent questions," Vic said.

"I got it. I'm free." Annalisa's blood pressure skyrocketed. One hand had wiggled free of the tie. She rubbed her wrist and hurried to untie her ankles. Then she untied Vic's feet and helped her to her feet.

"Okay," Annalisa said. "let me help get your ties off."

Vic's head shot up. "Footsteps," she mouthed. "Right outside."

Annalisa fumbled one plastic connection.

"Calm breaths," Vic whispered, "You can do this."

"Sure." She wiggled and pulled. And wiggled the tie off of Vic's wrist.

A key slid into the lock on the door.

"Weapons?" she mouthed at Vic's ear.

"Unzip the dress."

"Yea, shifters." Annalisa yanked the zipper down.

The deadbolt unlatched.

The artic fox was closer in size and demeanor to an enraged pit bull than a cute Disney cartoon fox. She leaped up on one of the higher shelves, knocking off rolls of toilet paper.

Darren, wearing a smug, over-confident expression on his face, pushed into the room. The fox growled. With teeth gleaming she dove for his throat.

* * *

Murdoch

Murdoch returned to the empty table with two over-flowing dinner plates. Where was everybody? Looking back to the food service, he spotted Ryan, next in line at the carving station. Too many guests had gone directly there, before the buffet. Where were Annalisa and Vic? He put the plates down and made a visual sweep of the entire ballroom. No mate.

He tried to sense her.

Not here, the dragon offered. All Murdoch could sense was the lack of his mate, her absence. Maybe because she wasn't a shifter? Or perhaps their bond was too new?

He didn't want to sit down at an empty table. He snuck a cherry tomato off the plate and popped it into his mouth. Looked over his shoulder. Ryan was balancing three plates, zigzagging across the room, hurrying toward him.

He put the plates down and leaned his grim face closer to Murdoch. "Darren has been here all evening, but hotel security just recently lost him. We need to get Vic and Annalisa back here. Now."

"Do we split up or stick together?" Murdoch was already headed to the door his mate had used earlier to leave the room.

"Together."

Murdoch pushed out of the ballroom.

Our mate is in danger.

"Appreciate the update," Murdoch snarked at the dragon. "Now find her."

Her aroma, Annalisa's unique combination of warn skin, shampoo, and light perfume, filled his nostrils.

"This way," he growled to Ryan.

There was a similar growl from a room just past the restrooms. Murdoch started running. Ryan drew his weapon and tried to keep pace.

When a firearm discharged inside the room, Murdoch went straight through the wooden door. And stopped on a dime.

Darren was flat on his back on the tile floor. Shallow puncture marks on his neck bled sluggishly. Standing on his chest was a big, seriously big, Arctic fox, snarling her warning. Murdoch's mate held a toilet plunger over her head, ready to clobber Darren.

Ryan pushed past him, gun at the ready, warning, "Nobody move."

"Chill, Ryan." Annalisa shook her plunger. "You too, honey. We got him. We outsmarted Darren and Vic captured him."

Murdoch stepped gingerly around Darren and the fox to take his mate in his arms. "Sweetling, you're sure you're not hurt?

"Not a scratch. But we need you two to take charge of Darren. Get him out of here so Vic can shift back and dress."

He dropped a kiss on Annalisa's head. "We heard a gunshot."

Annalisa pointed to a hole in the back wall. "When the fabulous fox went for his throat, stupid Darren shot the wall."

Murdoch looked to Ryan who was putting his weapon away. "What do we do with him?"

"Keep him locked down until you make the preemptive hoax announcement and Vic stops the auction. Everything is ready to go. Maybe the ballroom would be a good place for you to deny any Muirdris Shipping data leaks."

Murdoch winced when Annalisa pinched him. "Just take Darren outside, prop the door back in place, then go away," she said. "We'll meet you back at the table."

The fox sidestepped daintily off Darren's chest, and stood watching while he helped Ryan hoist the prisoner to his feet.

At the door, Ryan released a quiet whistle. "A vixen. Ultra-hot."

Chapter Twenty-Three

Annalisa shook out Vic's ball gown and helped her new best friend slide it on over her now human, naked body. The hotel storage room was eerily quiet after Murdoch propped the broken door back in place and left to help Ryan conceal Darren. She zipped up Vic's dress and gave her a quick hug. "This is my week for meeting new life-changing friends. Thank you for saving my life."

Vic hugged her back and shook her head. "You seem to forget your vital role in our escape. If you hadn't gotten both of us freed from those plastic ties, I never could've shifted. Thank you for saving my life."

"A team?"

"Deal. Now teammate, I'm starving. Do you figure we missed dinner?"

She lowered her voice, "I know a cute sea dragon who'd probably spring for steak dinners."

"Porterhouse rare and you're talking my language."

Annalisa and Vic edged past the broken door, and found Murdoch and Ryan waiting for them in the hallway.

"Hey. Nice surprise," Annalisa said pressed against Murdoch's solid chest. "But where's our traitor?"

Ryan held Vic's hand tightly. "I called a couple o'guys. Told 'em to babysit Darren 'til we finish cleaning up his mess. Then, unless the bomber implicates him, he'll go free."

Annalisa shot Ryan a deep frown. "That doesn't seem fair after all the—"

"Free but knowing there's a big target on his back," Ryan assured her, "Which will be used if he ever messes with Muirdris Shipping or any of her staff again."

"As you see," Murdoch said, "Ryan has everything well in hand. I'm here only because I couldn't bear to be away from my new fiancé. And I have one more duty to perform. A brief public announcement assuring the world that all of the Muirdris data is inviolate, and all aspects of our operations remain secure. At the same time, Vic will stop the auction."

"I've got the commands ready to be sent," Vic said, "through a remote server."

"The woman's a genius," Ryan murmured.

"Then," Murdoch continued, "if there's any food left, we eat. If not, we can order up dinner to the suite here in the hotel. Or Vic, you are welcome to helicopter back to our home, and join us and Ryan for a late dinner there."

"Our home. That sounds lovely," Annalisa sighed against his shoulder.

"New mates," Vic warned. "They'll be all lovey-dovey like this for months."

"For the rest of our lives," Murdoch assured his mate and their friends. "Now, let's get this done."

In the ballroom, their table had been cleared, but the celebration was in full swing with all the attendees still dancing, chatting, and drinking.

"You sure know how to throw a party," Annalisa whispered to Murdoch as the head waiter approached them.

"Sir," he bowed to Murdoch, "if you and your guests are ready to eat, I'm able to replicate the food on the plates we removed."

"Excellent." Murdoch smiled up at him. "Bring those as soon as they're ready. And tell the orchestra leader I'll be making a few remarks after they finish this set."

"Yes, sir. That'll be two more songs. A pleasure serving you, sir."

Ryan's phone buzzed. "It's Alice from the ship-yard," he said and hurried to a corner of the ballroom, completed the call, and returned slowly.

"What's wrong?" Annalisa asked.

"Nothing really," Ryan said, then lowered his voice. "The bomber's body was recovered. They'll per-form an autopsy, but it looks like drowning. The guy in custody confessed to bombing the garage at Muir-dris headquarters and to his part in the attempted bombing of the new ship. Seems the two men are cous-ins, and he claims there's no one else involved. Both are ex-employees of Muirdris. The deceased cousin fired for drinking on the job. The surviving man for fighting. He denies any connection to Darren."

"That's pretty clear-cut," Murdoch said.

"But why in hell would Darren betray the com-pany?" Ryan said. "Nobody saw that coming."

Murdoch lowered his voice. "Your men are hav-ing an informal talk with Darren right now, recording it, right?"

"Yes, so maybe we'll know more later."

Murdoch made his 'few remarks' from the orches-tra platform and as he spoke, Annalisa warmed with pride. Even better than the press conference, tonight he held his audience entranced, in a very human way. This time he could be less formal. His guests laughed and applauded during his talk.

Across the table, Vic sat with her phone ready. Midway through Murdoch's speech, he nodded to Vic, she pushed Send, and her part of the mission was complete.

After Murdoch finished, he made his way back to her, slowing only to shake hands and accept congratulations.

Dinner was delicious, and her dessert was positively decadent.

"Shall we dance?" Murdoch asked, grinning at her.

"Definitely. I need to work off this meal."

An hour later, the dance floor was still crowded. Annalisa swayed in Murdoch's arms to a slow song. Resting her head on his chest, she said, "It's been an unforgettable day and night. And it's beginning to catch up to me. Could we go home now?"

Murdoch guided her back to their table where Vic and Ryan sat deep in conversation.

"We're going home," Murdoch told them, "You're both invited to—"

"No thanks, boss," Ryan said. "I'm escorting Vic home, then driving back later tonight. I assigned one of our house guards to fly with you. Nexia was already working here tonight."

Nexia, their substitute bodyguard, met them at the ballroom exit and escorted them to the roof and into the helicopter. Annalisa drifted to sleep in the chopper and blinked awake when Murdoch laid her on his bed.

"Aren't we sleeping on the hoard?" she murmured.

"You, Annalisa Bartello, my eternal Sweetling, are the most beautiful creature ever born. Smart, resilient, and full of unexpected and wondrous talents, you're the ideal partner. And now you're talking about bedding down with your love-sick sea dragon on his hoard? Definitely, the perfect mate. I love you. I'll treasure and adore you forever."

"Show me."

*   *   *

Murdoch

Murdoch woke late the next morning, with his beloved mate tucked securely in his arms. He loved watching her sleep. As if on cue, she stirred and opened her eyes.

"Morning."

"Good morning," he said and kissed her forehead. "Do you want an update on Darren now or after I feed you breakfast?"

"Now, please."

"Ryan sent us a private message. He doesn't want Vic hurt by Darren's twisted motivations."

"What?"

"At some point last night, Darren realized he was being detained while his auction was cancelled. He totally lost it. Went off in a psychotic rant to Ryan's men. It quickly became obvious, Darren secretly despises women. He particularly hated working for Vic. He was even disgusted by the fact she shortened her name. The man is mentally ill, and Ryan doesn't want Vic blaming herself for the theft of the protocols. Also, he wanted to confirm Muirdris would cover psychiatric help for Darren."

"And you agreed?

"I did. I don't want you worrying about Darren, either. He's going to get help. You and I have a busy day ahead."

"Wait a minute," she said. "You've been up already? Working?"

"Dragon's honor, I came straight back to bed after getting the Mykos offer outlined. It's a complicated assignment I need to wrap up. Oh, and I read Ryan's message."

"Honey, that wasn't a criticism. Still, I'm feeling like a slacker."

"Sweetling, you're officially off work…"

Annalisa glanced up at him, her sharp eyes searching. Still, she waited while he fidgeted. He'd finished writing the Mykos offer and wanted a second set of eyes. Her eyes and her opinion. Just say it.

"Even though you're not working today, would you read through the offer? Double check I didn't miss anything?"

"I'd be happy to. With the clear understanding that I've never worked procurement."

"Thank you."

"Um, you said busy day, which scares me," she teased. "What else is on your agenda?"

"I want to announce our engagement today." He couldn't wait to tell the world. However, he suspected his mate had a mental check-list to complete first. She threaded her finger through his. Here it comes.

"Do we need to clear that with HR?"

An easy question. "Depends on who you'll be working for." He kept his tone casual while he tracked her body language like a bird of prey.

"I've given it some thought," she said, equally laid-back. "Finnian's a great boss to work for and I'm enjoying all my projects and the new assignments."

"All right…" he said. Shit, shit. No, give her a minute.

"My first choice is to stay on Finnian's team if I can live here in Massachusetts and telecommute."

His heart soaring, Murdoch let out a whoop and pounced, kissing her until they were both gasping for air. "You are beyond perfect," he wheezed. It didn't help that the dragon was dancing an Irish jig.

"I didn't fool you for a minute," she grumbled. "You know I can't leave you."

"And I feel exactly the same way."

"While you're in a mellow mood, *I* have two favors to ask concerning the engagement announcement."

"As my beautiful mate would say, 'Uh oh'."

"Let's not make it public until you tell Murphy."

"Done. What else?"

"While we wait for Murphy to come home, would you figure out another proposal? One that isn't quite so X-rated?"

"Like asking you in a restaurant?" Dull stuff. Kneeling on the hoard had been traditional, classic.

"Think about it," she said. "One day our children are going to ask how you proposed to me. I don't want to tell them I was spread out naked on the hoard. We need to create an alternate story."

"For our future children?"

"Yes." His mate looked positively adorable with flushed, pink cheeks.

"I'll get right to work on that."

"Terrific. How about we shower and dress, then you bring a copy of the Mykos offer, while I make coffee? We can meet in the breakfast nook."

The shower took even longer than he'd anticipated. Still, based on her moans of satisfaction echoing off the tile walls, his mate thoroughly enjoyed the extra time and attention.

He brought his laptop to the kitchen and set it down in front of her.

"French toast?" he asked.

She was already peering intently at the document on the screen. "Uh huh," she mumbled.

Ten minutes later, her head came up and she looked at him over the computer screen. "Murdoch, you're such a dog in the manger. This offer is awesome. You didn't miss a trick. You wanted me to read it so I could applaud, pat you on the back."

"No, I... Well, I was hoping I'd nailed it."

"You absolutely did. Mykos wants to sell everything, right? And you're only going for the break-even and profitable parts of their company?"

"Brilliant woman," he said. "We're only buying what we can use, or we walk. It's a strong position."

She jumped up, ran around the table, and leapt into his arms. "You're such a great businessman. And so sexy when you talk negotiations."

"Mind the spatula." He stepped back from the gas range and groped her butt while he kissed her. "I love you."

"Me too."

"Let's get plenty of food in us. Then we can go back to bed and teach each other every negotiating trick we know."

ACKNOWLEDGEMENTS

I wish to thank my family for the years of unwavering support and encouragement.

Thanks to my critique partner Elaine Calloway for keeping me on track, for catching the parts where I tended to get carried away,

A special thank you to my new series editor Cheryl Barnes-Neff for knowing and enforcing all those pesky structure, grammar, and punctuation rules while being supportive and constructive at the same time.

Many thanks to Sharon Lipman at Fantasia Covers for a beautiful series logo, and a new set of awesome covers.

ABOUT THE AUTHOR

CJ Matthew, multi-published romance author, is introducing a new paranormal romance series, *Sea Dragon Shifters* for 2019. Book 1, *Murdoch*, introduces the Irish clan of sea dragons posing as humans and running their international conglomerate, Muirdris Shipping. CJ grew up in an Air Force family that travelled all over the U.S. and around the world. She spent her high school and university years living in California, which inspired her love of marine life and the Pacific Ocean. And she loves to write about cities worldwide.

A member of Georgia Romance Writers (GRW) Romance Writers of America, CJ lives and writes near a lake in the woods northeast of Atlanta. When she isn't writing or reading romances, CJ likes to travel and to spend time with her two grown children, a brilliant grandson and a feisty cat named Max.

Thank you for reading *Murdoch*. **Would you like to read the next book? Devlin, Sea Dragon Shifter Book 2** is available on Amazon Kindle Unlimited or in paperback.

Reminder: each book in all of CJ's series can stand alone, they don't need to be read in any order, and there are no cliffhangers.

PLEASE! Leave a review!
If you liked Murdoch, tell your friends! And reviews help readers find new books and authors that are right for them. Please leave a review on Amazon, on Good-Reads, and your favorite book review site.

Want to be friends? Find CJ at:
Facebook: "Like" the page:
https://www.facebook.com/CJMatthewauthor
Website: www.cjmatthew.com
Be sure to sign up for the Newsletter.
Twitter: https://www.twitter.com/cjmatthew
Amazon author page: "Follow CJ" at:
https://www.amazon.com/author/cjmatthew
Goodreads: "Follow CJ" at:
https://www.goodreads.com/CJMatthew

Printed in Great Britain
by Amazon

61889790R00139